Russell Wangersky's most recent book, *The Glass Harmonica*, won the 2010 Winterset Award and was long-listed for the Relit Awards. His previous book, *Burning Down the House: Fighting Fires and Losing Myself*, won the British Columbia National Award for Canadian Non-Fiction, the Rogers Communications Newfoundland and Labrador Non-Fiction Book Award, and the Edna Staebler Award for Creative Non-Fiction. It was also a finalist for the Writer's Trust Non-Fiction Prize and was a *Globe and Mail* Top 100 selection in 2008. His 2006 short story collection, *The Hour of Bad Decisions*, was long-listed for the Scotiabank Giller Prize and was short-listed for the Commonwealth Writer's Prize, First Book, Canada and the Caribbean. It was a *Globe and Mail* Top 100 selection in 2006. Wangersky lives and works in St. John's, where he is an editor and columnist with the *St. John's Telegram*.

Books of Merit

WHIRL AWAY

ALSO BY RUSSELL WANGERSKY

The Hour of Bad Decisions
Burning Down the House
The Glass Harmonica

Whirl
AWAY

RUSSELL WANGERSKY

THOMAS ALLEN PUBLISHERS
TORONTO

Copyright © 2012 Russell Wangersky

All rights reserved. No part of this work may be reproduced or
transmitted in any form or by any means—graphic, electronic, or
mechanical, including photocopying, recording, taping, or information
storage and retrieval systems—without the prior written permission
of the publisher, or in the case of photocopying or other reprographic
copying, a licence from the Canadian Copyright Licensing Agency.

Library and Archives Canada Cataloguing in Publication

Wangersky, Russell, 1962–
Whirl away / Russell Wangersky.

Short stories.

ISBN 978-0-88762-936-5

I. Title.

PS8645.A5333W55   2012   c813'.6   C2011-907120-7

Editor: Janice Zawerbny
Cover design: Michel Vrána
Cover image: John Krempl/photocase.com

Published by Thomas Allen Publishers,
a division of Thomas Allen & Son Limited,
390 Steelcase Road East,
Markham, Ontario L3R 1G2 Canada

www.thomasallen.ca

The publisher gratefully acknowledges the support of
The Ontario Arts Council for its publishing program.

We acknowledge the support of the Canada Council for the Arts, which last
year invested $20.1 million in writing and publishing throughout Canada.

We acknowledge the Government of Ontario through the Ontario
Media Development Corporation's Ontario Book Initiative.

We acknowledge the financial support of the Government of Canada
through the Canada Book Fund for our publishing activities.

12 13 14 15 16   5 4 3 2 1

Text printed on a 100% PCW recycled stock

Printed and bound in Canada

For Leslie, who whirls.

CONTENTS

WHIRL AWAY

BOLT

THE BOLT came through the open back window of the truck. It came in end over end. From a distance, if anyone had been watching it, concentrating, it might actually have appeared that the truck was doing the tumbling, and that the bolt was flying perfectly straight.

Just a rusty bolt John had found in the driveway, a bolt that he'd tossed in the back of the pickup with the duffle bags and the mitre saw and the rest of his stuff.

He didn't hear the bolt whisper as it spun, the rushing air whistling along the even gaps of the threads; he had his hands full trying to figure out just what was happening to the pickup as it cut through the bright pink flowering fireweed, the truck leaving a four-wheeled, mown trail behind it, the wheels throwing up grass and mud and the petals of the flowers.

The bolt caught him in the curve at the back of his skull, at the midline and just below his hair, hitting that smooth dent where a lover might rest the heel of her hand. John had a brief moment to think about what-if—what if he hadn't reached across the seat towards the glove compartment, what if he hadn't over-corrected when the wheels touched the shoulder. He didn't even get to "What if I hadn't put the bolt in the back?" or more importantly, "Why did it fly so straight?" or "What are the chances of that happening?"

The bolt was still moving at close to a hundred kilometres an hour, the same speed the truck had been going before the front end smashed nose first into the bank. John, safely held in the grasp of the seat belt, had slowed as quickly as the truck had. He didn't feel the bolt hit.

John, for once, didn't feel anything at all.

The truck ended up on its roof, one wheel crookedly spinning long after the other three had stopped, and no one noticed the wreck until the next morning. Then a long-haul driver, riding high up in the cab of his Freightliner, saw the rusting bottom of the chassis standing out against the green and pink of the fireweed, rectangular and ochre and perched on the edge of a small peaty stream. There was already cold dew on the windshield when the driver waded down through the high plants to look through the window on the driver's side.

"John was coming home," Bev said.

"No, he wasn't."

"Yes he was, bitch. He was on his way here when he crashed. He was coming home for good. Why do you think he had all his stuff?"

"You're lying." Anne said the words quickly, as if saying them could force the doubt away, but she heard the tremble in her own voice—and she hated herself for betraying that feeling, even slightly. Because she hadn't known where he was going. Sleeping, caught up in the false, warm security of comforter, sheets and pillow, she hadn't even realized he had left.

They were speaking in undertones, barely more than hissing the words, aware that there were other people in the funeral home but focused on each other. Outside, the sun had come out around a huge grey bank of cloud, and individual shafts of sunlight were sifting down onto the surface of Bay Bulls, lighting irregular, ragged patches of ocean as if the light actually meant to single something out amongst the choppy grey waves.

Bev was small and blond and strangely angular. She gave the sense of always having her elbows in close to her sides and her hands up high, as if spoiling for a fight. That, and she finished her sentences by pushing her face forwards, like she was punctuating her words with her chin, daring the other person to disagree. It was the sort of habit that some people found off-putting, as much of a shove as if she had reached out and pushed them with both hands palm-flat against their chest.

Whenever she saw Bev, whenever she spoke with the other woman, Anne was always left with the same disconcerting thought: just how had John ever ended up married to her? It made her wonder if there was some kind of hidden, underlying character flaw in him that she knew nothing about, or that she was trying to ignore.

When she asked John about it, after they'd moved in together, he would shrug. "I was young, okay?" he would say, as if that was excuse enough. "We were both young."

But she found that hard to accept—trying to imagine how it was that someone as easygoing as John would choose to marry someone so abrasive. Other people offered up old sayings like "Opposites attract," but Anne couldn't see it.

"No, really," she'd ask him. "How'd you even get in the same room with each other, let alone end up married?" And John would do what he always did, pushing his hands through the hair at his temples, where it grew coarser and with slightly more curl than on the rest of his head. It was a motion that always dislodged flecks of fugitive sawdust from the day's work with the sander or fine curls of shavings from the planer. There was always sawdust on him somewhere, Anne knew, fragrant small chips that gave him an unexpected air of solidity, the green of birch, the closer, sticky familiarity of pine—a smell that was as much him as any other. He'd push his hands through his hair once or twice every time, but it was a way of saying that he wouldn't answer, that the conversation was done. It was a signal that he was about to shut down. It was the one thing about him that she found infuriating—the ability to stop any discussion by withdrawing completely. He'd always done it, even before they'd moved into the old green house on the side of the hill, before he'd put up the new clapboard and trim on the outside, before he'd taken every single window down and replaced it with a new one. Before he'd built the walkway and the tidy, hiphigh white fence with the gate and the big deck where they sometimes sat late into the night and looked out over the water at the wide white strip of reflected moonlight.

From the house, Anne could look across the flat bay and see the cream-coloured, weathered side of Bev's house, the blue car nose down in the driveway, and she imagined that Bev got up every morning and saw exactly what she saw too, only in reverse. Bev would have to look out over the metal grey of the bay and see John and Anne's house, and her mouth would tighten.

Lives like a mirror, Anne thought. Exactly like a mirror—every reflection an opposite. Where Bev was hard, Anne knew she was soft. Bev has angles, Anne thought, standing naked in front of the mirror; Bev has angles where I have curves. Bev has no give to her, and I, well, I always give.

Bev's house was on the north side of the harbour, Anne and John's on the south, but both houses were high up above the water in timothy meadow—both hills bright green in the spring, straw yellow by mid-August.

So much the same, she thought, but so very different.

Anne wondered if the other woman ever even came close to seeing what she did when she stood outside the house; whether Bev saw the simple roses tangling in the ditch by the road, the alder catkins turning slowly through waxy hard green to brown. Whether she actually smelled the same wind, felt the same smooth surface of beach rocks between her thumb and forefinger. Somehow, Anne couldn't imagine that she did, couldn't imagine that Bev actually framed anything more than practical thoughts.

"Would you have left if she hadn't?" Anne asked late one night, her fingers gently touching the line of dark, curly hair that ran down from his navel to his crotch. John hadn't answered at first, not until she pressed him. "Would you?"

"Probably."

And while she didn't doubt that it was true, it wasn't anywhere near the answer she had wanted to hear. She wanted to punch him and say, "No, you dope. You say, 'I would have left her, just to look for you.' That's what you say."

But she didn't, and by then he was sleeping anyway.

There was lots of work that year, much more than when John and Bev had eked out a living on Bev's teaching salary and piecemeal carpentry work. John had been able to build the workshop by the harbour by the time he started living with Anne, and the shop was alternately busy with mundane work—installing cabinets here, pulling out rotten windows and replacing them with vinyl there—and the more involved projects in a small town, such as building new kitchens and pulling out entire rotten floors. She loved to hear about the tearing out, when John would come home with tufts of wet, rotten wood in the wrinkles of his clothes, with the rich, wet smell all around, pulling out small treasures to show her. A big round copper penny found caught behind a baseboard, or great long cut nails, every one of them over a hundred years old, solid and sharp and, she knew, not handled even once between the time they had been pounded into place and when John had pulled them out again. Anne loved the way he would open his big battered hands slowly, gently, as if he were about to reveal something as fragile as a flower or a small bird tossed from its nest, the way he would show her something both simple and complex that he knew she was going to understand.

At times like that, she felt as if they had a unique connection, as if there was something between them that no one else knew, that they were lovers in a way neither of them had shared before with anyone.

It was the same feeling she believed they shared over the big jobs, the occasional work that brought special, expensive wood to the work shed, jobs that seemed, in their own way, to reveal some part of John as clearly as when he brought something back to show her.

John had built a custom dining room table for the president of the electric company—a man with more money than taste, John joked, but he loved the work intensely. The table was an oval sweep of light birch, the thread of the grain matched with precision and hours of careful work, the top glassy with varnish. Then he'd gotten the contract for an even bigger table, for the utility's boardroom.

Anne had brought his lunch down to the shop every day while he was working on the big table. She had caught him looking along the grain, his face a serious, complicated map, and when he'd seen her and straightened up, rubbing his hands on a piece of cloth, his eyes changed, like someone moving quickly away from the edge of a window and letting the curtains fall back into place.

"I don't know if I can give it up," he said, and for a moment she felt a skip in her chest. He must have seen the stricken look on her face. "The table," he explained. "I just don't know what it's going to be like not to have it here."

"That attached to it, are you?" she asked.

"It's not that. It's just that . . . It's just that sometimes people don't deserve things, even if they can afford them."

Outside, the raspberry bushes were August high against the converted shed, and the wind coming off the bay made the canes switch back and forth gently across the exterior clapboard with a rhythmic, constant scrape. Some people might find it irritating, Anne thought as they stood there. John didn't even seem to notice it, and to her, it was as regular and reassuring as waking up in the black of night and hearing John's breathing beside her: regular, deep in his chest, her lover asleep flat on his back and completely unaware that she was even there.

In the end, the big table went anyway. John had to get the movers to come and take it in the big van, in sections, and then he spent an afternoon at the utility's head office, putting the sections together and tightening all the screws and fasteners. When he was finished, it was like a single piece of a huge tree, as if it had taken root there in the boardroom and grown.

"If they ever have to move it," he said seriously to the receptionist on the executive floor, "tell them to call me. I'll come right in. It's strong enough in one piece, but you can't go dragging it around. It's not made for that."

That night, they went out to celebrate at the Eagle, although Anne wasn't sure whether it would turn out to be a celebration or a wake; John had a way of drinking just enough to topple sharply off a cliff into misery, even when everything seemed fine. One moment they could be laughing and the next he might be lashing out, a spiteful drunk for no clear reason she could fathom. And when they went into the lounge, she had a feeling it would be one of those nights, especially because Bev was at the bar with an after-hours group of other teachers. All the other teachers except Kevin, the grade four teacher Bev had left John for. Kevin, who had lasted all of five months before Bev had suddenly decided she wanted her quiet carpenter back.

But by then it was too late. John always said it was as if he had hardened into something quite different than he had been. That he had cured quickly, like two-stage epoxy glue mixed together. There was, Anne knew, a certain flintiness about him now; Anne would run into it occasionally, abruptly, especially in the dark moments when John had had two or three drinks too many, or worse, when the work dried up and even the deep cuts on his hands had a chance to heal over. There was a great wide seam of distrust in there, Anne knew, and it was always unpleasant when she struck it.

In the bar, Anne stared across at Bev and the other teachers, and wondered what John had ever seen in the small woman. Damn, Anne thought, looking at Bev's rigid back, she even sits like a block of wood. That almost made Anne laugh out loud. A few ryes too many, she thought, trying to hold back the giggles. A piece of wood—she knew exactly why John would have been attracted to that. Drill here, plane there, she thought, and then she was laughing, shoulders shaking, face down on the table next to her glass. And then John was back from the bathroom, and the band was starting again. He grabbed her hands, pulled her up out of her seat towards the dance floor.

Anne was sweating and strangely elated when she stopped dancing and pushed her way through the swinging door into the women's washroom. Late by then, and the bar was full of cigarette smoke and noise—the stalls all full, and Angie Porter, barely old enough to even be in the bar, was fixing her makeup in the mirror.

"Hi, Ange," Anne said.

Angie turned and put a finger to her lips, pointing to one of the stall doors. "Bev," she mouthed.

Anne shrugged. "So what?" she said loudly. Too many ryes for sure, she thought, hearing how roughly the words came out.

The toilet flushed and Bev came out of the stall, almost walking right into Anne.

"Looks like they'll let anyone in here," Bev said, her chin up.

"Looks like," Anne said. "You're here."

Then Bev slapped her—hard. Angie fled the washroom, banging the door back into the wall as she hurried out. Anne's hand came up to the side of her face instinctively, feeling the heat welling up under her skin.

When she came out of the bathroom, her face still throbbing, Bev was gone.

"You gotta tell me," she said to John later, after the moon had risen huge and orange and then had fallen back away behind the horizon. They were walking, climbing slowly back up the hill, holding hands, weaving slightly.

Anne looked back over her shoulder at the one yellow light that was still on in Bev's house, one yellow light like a hard, staring eye.

"What?" John answered.

"You've got to tell me how the two of you ended up married," Anne said. "You have to tell me how the heck that could happen."

"It just did."

"That's not an answer. That's an excuse."

"Maybe it was her idea," John said, and Anne could see he had already brought one hand up to the small curls on the side of his head. "Maybe we were together a lot, dating in high school, and it seemed like a good idea, like it was the natural thing to do."

"Like, 'Oh well, here we are, might as well get married'?" Anne asked, incredulous. "No one gets married because it's just the easiest thing to do."

"Whatever you like," John said. "You asked."

The higher they climbed towards the house, the more the lights of the rest of Bay Bulls nestled down into a bowl beneath them. It looked as if all of the houses would fit into two cupped hands, like tight bunches of bundled Christmas lights.

"What was it like, with her?" Anne asked. "It couldn't have all been bad. There must have been a time when everything was clicking. A time when you were happy."

John shrugged—not like he didn't know how to answer, but like he knew exactly what to say but was refusing to say it. "S'ppose," he said, sounding resigned. "Jeez. Sometimes you sound just like her."

Anne felt her breath stop, the muscles in her chest rigid and fixed like they might never move again. Like she'd been hit again.

John had let go of her hand and was still walking, the distance growing between them. Anne forced herself to walk again, forced herself to start breathing, trying to find a place to hold on to in a suddenly tilting world. The sky was alive with stars then, so Anne looked up at the wide, broad sweep of the Milky Way, deliberately trying to wonder if every one of the stars already had its name. Then she'd caught up, and John took her hand again as if nothing had happened, and the sky rushed back away from her and settled into its proper place.

John reached out and opened the gate at the end of the walkway, and the hinges squeaked just like they always did. Later, Anne would remember that it was the last time before the accident that she could recall actually looking—really looking—at his hands.

Ten days later, after the accident, she was packing up the last scattered pieces of his things, and almost absentmindedly turned on his cellphone. The police had returned the phone to her, along with his tool belt and the mitre saw and the rest of the tools and bags of clothes from the back of the pickup. Almost immediately, the phone rang. The ringing startled her, but she answered it anyway.

"John there?" a hollow man's voice said.

"Ah, no," Anne said, flustered.

"Well, where the hell is he?" the man asked. "He was supposed to be out here a week ago."

"Where's here?"

"Brooks. Brooks, Alberta." The man on the other end of the phone sounded exasperated. "Look, I got him the damned job—sure, I know he's way overqualified for framing work—but I got him the damned job and now he's making me look bad for recommending him in the first place. He was supposed to start four days ago. When the hell's he going to get here, anyway?"

The cellphone dropped out of her hand while she was looking across at Bev's house on the other side of the bay. It was dark, and she was startled to see her own face reflected back in the window glass.

And for a moment, lying face up on the hardwood floor, the phone kept squeaking and whistling, like a small bird desperate for home.

ECHO

KEVIN ROWE was on the front deck, hemmed in behind the fence pickets, looking down on the narrow street.

He was five years old, and he had serious, obvious eyes with small, square eyeglasses. Behind the glasses, emotions played across his face quickly, like a travelling storm. His eyebrows rose at the faintest hint of confusion, furrowing his forehead, and fell again quickly, leaving behind a blank, smooth slate that seemed never to have borne a mark. He had short hair, all of it cut the same length so that it stood up like bristles on a brush.

Kevin was just tall enough that his eyes were above the level of the deck railing, sharp blue eyes that didn't seem to blink often enough. He stared, unabashed, at passing cars, at walking people.

And he talked in short, tight bursts of words.

"Don't you care what I think?" he said over the edge of the railing, the movement of his lips barely visible but his mouth enunciating every word. "Don't you even care what I think?"

The railing topped the brown fence that ran all the way around the deck, and all the way around the front of the small bungalow.

It was a white house, vinyl siding, single storey with light blue trim, occasional brushstrokes of blue lipping onto the white like bent feathers. All the windows of the small dark bedrooms at the front of the house were open, doing their best to shed the heat. It was uncomfortably hot for St. John's, the air thick and heavy and motionless. All-over damp, like the inside of Kevin's father's work gloves, when he had taken them off for a rest and Kevin had slid one of his own hands inside.

Kevin's parents were in the kitchen at the back, his father sitting down at the table with his work shirt off, his undershirt going yellow, his mother doing dishes in the steel sink. Kevin didn't like the sound of the dishes, the way the plates and cutlery rattled and scraped against the metal.

Before he went out, he had brought his bowl over to the sink the way he was supposed to, a scant handful of cereal Os swimming like life rings in the leftover milk. The handle of the spoon slid back and forth along the edge of the bowl with every step.

Then his mother told Kevin to go out on the deck. His father was looking down at his feet as if he was surprised they were still in the same place.

Kevin's father drove from St. John's to Boston and back, big rigs with chrome wheels, and every time he came home,

Kevin would come into the living room and be startled to find his father in front of the television or hear his father in the bedroom, snoring, like he'd never really left. For Kevin, it was like going into the kitchen and finding there was an extra fridge where there hadn't been one before. It was a magic trick, as if his father could just simply appear, again and again and again. By the time the surprise of it wore off, Kevin's father would be ready to head back out on the road, hauling fish to Boston and furniture back again.

Kevin's mother held the door open as he went out onto the deck, telling him not to get into trouble. "Stay on the deck and stay off the road," she said, and as she did, a car whooshed by next to the deck, like an example she'd whipped up just for him.

"Stay off the road," she said again, and she put all the emphasis on "off."

Kevin heard the door latch behind her, the click sharp and final.

Kevin's father hadn't said anything when Kevin was in the kitchen, but a few moments later Kevin heard the deep rumble of his voice from the kitchen, not so much words as a deep straight line, all one note. And over the top of it, his mother's thin voice, growing higher and then falling away like a ball bouncing up and down, up and down. It was like they were singing together, each one already sure where the other was going and just exactly where they would eventually end up.

It was hot in the sun, Kevin thought, and the water in the inflatable swimming pool on the deck was murky, catching struggling daddy-long-legs and wandering, curious, paper-winged moths that lay flat on the surface, at the mercy of potential rescuers. It was too late for several toys, completely submerged and fuzzed with small air bubbles.

Kevin fished the toys out—a green rubber frog that sprayed water out through a small hole in its mouth, a plastic power shovel, the hard yellow wand from a bottle of bubble liquid—making sure he kept the dripping water away from his T-shirt and shorts, and then threw them back in again, watching them sink back down to the blue vinyl bottom of the pool.

After he threw them back in, they lay still on the bottom. Above them, the ripples on the surface made them appear to wriggle for a few moments before the water fell still. The bottom of the pool had lines where the weight of the water had pulled the plastic down into the cracks between the boards.

"There you go again," Kevin said to the surface of the water. "There you go again. How many times do I have to listen to this stuff?"

He turned, and out on the road he saw a man with a dog on a leash. The dog was brown and white, a heavy, low-slung beagle with big, sad, bloodshot eyes and dragging ears. Kevin thought that the dog and the man looked a lot alike, and he watched them through the slatted pickets as they made their way along the road.

He pressed himself down onto the surface of the deck, trying to make himself inconspicuous, creeping on his stomach so that he stayed even with the dog's slow, plodding walk. The street ran in tight to the front of the deck, so Kevin could look through the railing and see the mottled colour of the side of the man's face, dappled with small, shiny beads of sweat.

The man looked angry, Kevin thought, even though there was nothing to be angry about.

Suddenly, there were seeds from dandelions parachuting in on the wind under their silver-white canopies, regiments of soldiers, landing all around him, and Kevin was the only one left to protect the base, the only survivor.

"Bang!" he said, pointing a loaded index finger at the air.

The dog looked around at the sound and stopped walking, but the man kept going, pulling the leash hard. The dog appeared startled when the collar suddenly dug into its neck.

"Save it for someone who cares," Kevin said to the dog. "Save it for someone who cares."

The dog didn't look back.

Across the street, Mrs. Batten came around the corner of her house from the backyard and started to rake the grass. Rake, rake, stop. Rake, rake, stop.

During one of the stops, she looked across, spotted Kevin and waved. But Kevin wasn't sure whose army she was with, whether she knew the password or not, so he kept very still and looked up under the edge of the railing, watching for airplanes. Everyone has to watch for the planes. It was like that in every movie.

Sometimes, airplanes draw lines with clouds, Kevin thought, like arrows that show you right where they are. And sometimes, they make a noise that makes you think they're actually somewhere else, not where they are.

Then he saw there was a spider in the corner of the deck, a brown, fat spider with a white pattern on its backside. The spider was finishing a small and perfect web under the top edge of the deck railing, the tips of its front legs plucking at the sticky lines, placing the threads.

Kevin pointed at the spider and shook his finger. "You don't want to fix things, do you? You don't even really want to try."

The spider continued picking at the sticky webbing, working its way around the outside circle of the web, Kevin's words passing right through it.

He sat down on the deck and watched the spider, pushing his glasses back up his nose every time they slid down. It was getting hotter on the deck, and he was starting to sweat.

Mrs. Batten finished raking and walked back behind her house, and Kevin purposefully watched her out of the corner of his eye.

Still, neither of his parents came to Kevin's front door. He thought they should, that someone should check to see what he was doing. The door was closed tight, like it was sealed into place. There were grown-up voices in the distance behind it, rumbling like a thunderstorm far away.

By then, the sun was high, and Kevin thought he would like a sandwich and some juice.

He would like a tuna fish sandwich on white bread, cut into triangles so that he could eat in from the points towards the crusts, and then leave the crusts behind on his plate. It would be even better if the bread was soft and fresh, so that he could flatten it into bread pills with his tongue against the roof of his mouth. And all the tuna, every scrap in the whole sandwich, would be light and pinkish and salty, with no fishy-tasting dark bits that pop up sometimes and wreck a whole sandwich.

Kevin thought he'd like a glass of apple juice, poured fast so that the bubbles stayed in place in a ring along the inside of the glass.

But there was no sandwich, and no apple juice.

Kevin watched the spider, and wondered if it would catch a fly and eat it. The web didn't look strong enough to hold anything, even if a fly accidently flew into the trap. "You'd like that, wouldn't you?" Kevin said sharply. "You'll go along with anything, as long as we're doing it your way."

Then there was the sharp sound of glass breaking inside the house, and from the front windows, loud voices that got louder every time the wind from the back of the house puffed the curtains out against the window screens. Now and then, Kevin could hear snatches of words, sometimes his mother, her voice low and hard and biting off the end of every word, his father's a steady grumble that sometimes erupted into single clear words like "job" and "paid." Once, a sound like someone smacking their hand flat down on the smooth surface of the countertop. Then, crying that sounded far away

to Kevin, like he was hearing it through a cardboard tube
from a roll of paper towels. The sounds kept rolling from the
house, like waves slapping in on the shore.

Kevin remembered the dog on the leash and wished he
had a dog. It wouldn't have to be a big dog, he thought, just a
friendly little dog with black eyes and a wet nose, the kind of
dog that would drink water from the swimming pool and
then look out through the fence with him. They could ex-
plore the back of the house and the bottom of the sharp cliff,
and all the time the dog would be busy with its nose, head
down and curious. Kevin thought he would let the dog sleep
in his room, up on the foot of his bed if it wanted, and if there
was ever a fire or burglars, the dog would wake up and lift its
head and growl deep in his throat as a warning. After the first
time the dog warned them about something dangerous, his
parents would let the dog sleep anywhere it wanted.

After a while, Kevin found the last part of the deck where
there was still a long blue triangle of shade, and he fell asleep
on the boards watching a line of ants march around the
corner of the house and down the siding to the ground.
Just before he slept, Kevin was thinking about what kind of
name his dog would have.

When he woke up, the sun had toppled over the cliff
behind the house and the whole deck was in shadow. It was
colder, and there was a white and blue police car parked on
the road, the lights on its roof flashing and throwing the
shadows of the fence palings across him and all around the
front of the house.

A policeman got out of the car and closed the door. Then he walked up to the deck, reaching over the top of the gate so he could open the latch from the inside.

He nodded at Kevin and put one finger in front of his lips, but he didn't say anything. Kevin nodded back, and he thought the policeman smiled, but he wasn't sure. The policeman's face was pulled tight.

Kevin sat up, resting his back against the fence, and watched as the policeman reached a hand out for the door-knob and turned it without even knocking. The policeman's other hand was on top of the gun in his holster. Kevin could see the black butt end of the gun, its plastic handle patterned and rough. That's so you can get a good grip on it, he thought. So you can hold on tight when you shoot.

The policeman held on to his gun, although he didn't take it out of the holster, and with his other hand he pushed the door open and went in, the door angling closed behind him.

Kevin stood up, looked across the street and saw Mrs. Batten looking out through the front window of her house, but she only stayed there for a second. All along the street, Kevin saw people in their doorways, as if they were listening to some distant sound, like a mysterious silent dog whistle. He saw the way the neighbours were all tilting their heads, all turning a little bit the same way. He saw the Barretts and even Mrs. Connaught, who sometimes brought warm cookies over to his house on a big colourful plate with a rooster on it.

Kevin thought he would like a cookie now.

Another police car arrived, and then another, a second policeman, then a third. The second policeman went into the house. The third one took Kevin's hand in his and pulled him in tight alongside the house.

"We'll just wait right here," the policeman said. He had short blond hair, and he sounded almost scared.

"Nothin' else on my dance card," Kevin said, his voice low and gruff. "Maybe you should just sit down and shut up for once."

The policeman looked at him and then towards the noises coming out of the house, but he didn't let go of Kevin's hand.

Soon, Kevin heard the rise and fall of a siren, getting closer and closer. By the time the ambulance swung wide around the narrow corner, all its lights flashing and taking up more than its own lane, there were people in almost every door along Fahey Street, and Mrs. Batten was standing on her lawn with both hands up in front of her mouth.

Kevin watched very carefully, without speaking or blinking. Watched as his father performed his disappearing act all over again, this time with his arms tight behind his back as if he was hiding something. The first policeman was holding on to his shoulder, as if he was trying to help him keep his balance. There were more policemen now, and there was a van. Inside the house, someone was taking photographs. Kevin could see the white flash from the camera bouncing off the walls.

He was thinking about tuna fish again. Then he thought that the ambulance attendants should be bringing the long white stretcher out and his mother should be reaching out from under the sheet and holding his hand for a moment before they took her through the gate to the ambulance.

"Be a good boy." That's what she would say, he decided. "Be a good boy and do what they tell you." Kevin was sure he would start to cry.

But his mother didn't come out, and the ambulance lights kept flashing, the back doors open so he could see inside.

Behind the police cars, a blue car with a serious-looking woman behind the steering wheel pulled up next to the fence. Kevin watched the car sitting at the curb.

"I'm Mrs. Thornhill," the woman said to Kevin after she climbed heavily up onto the deck next to him. "But you can call me Bo."

Bo had a folded grey blanket in her hands, and she unfolded it and put it over Kevin's shoulders. It was rough on his skin, and he shrugged it off the first time, but she put it back over him and led him to her car, where she put him in the back seat and fastened his seat belt.

"There you go, dear," she said.

Kevin didn't say anything.

Then she got into the front seat of the car and pulled her own seat belt across herself with a long, slow movement that looked difficult. It took a few tries before the tongue of the belt clicked into place. Then, Bo Thornhill said, "We're going to go for a ride. Here we go."

Kevin watched out the window, watched the way the pickets on the deck seemed to jump when the car started moving. He squinted his eyes, making the edges of the pickets flicker and go faster.

"Don't you care what I think?" he said to the smooth glass of the closed window as the lights started to hurry by, faster when his street joined a larger street and the car sped up.

He watched his breath fog on the inside of the glass when he said the words.

"Don't you even care?"

The inside of the car was still. When he listened carefully, it sounded like Bo Thornhill was humming quietly.

Then Kevin said: "Bitch."

After a moment, he added, "Just like your goddamn mother."

Up above, Kevin watched the flashing lights of a single airplane fingering the fading sky. The sound of its engines hadn't caught up yet, he thought, because it was still stretched out behind it across the air.

McNALLY'S FAIR

DENNIS MEANEY was painting The Thunder apple green—a brilliant green that would make the roller coaster stand out even when the spring had brought the prairie into that brief emerald flush before the sun got around to browning it over. It wasn't the colour he would have chosen. Mr. Reinhoudt had picked the colour, even though Dennis told him just looking at the paint samples hurt his eyes.

"Is s'pposed to," Mr. Reinhoudt said, pulling hard on his small white beard. "S'pposed to get yer attention from the highway, and getcha in the lot wit' the kids." He said "kids" as if it had a *z* in it.

Reinhoudt was a small, round, compact Dutchman who'd spent twenty years building the amusement park he'd named McNally's Fair, because, he said, McNally was a more acceptable name than his own. The Zipper first, then bumper cars; a small, brightly lit merry-go-round, and a Ferris wheel that picked awkward times to slip out of gear. Reinhoudt bought them one at a time, with careful, calculating precision. He'd bought The Zipper from a travelling fair when its semi-hauler broke down on the highway on the way to Swift Current and it looked to its old owners as if a new rig would cost more than the whole ride was worth all together.

Reinhoudt's park was twenty minutes west of Calgary, and The Thunder was the main attraction, a short, steep roller coaster that got riders high enough to give them a clear view, on the right day, of the foothills below the Rocky Mountains. Dennis was the only full-time employee outside the Reinhoudt family, and he thought that explained just what kind of jobs he ended up doing—the worst of them. Even Michaela, Reinhoudt's daughter, had a better job than he did—Michaela Reinhoudt, in her twenties now and distant, no longer the same teenager playing at talking rough, hanging out with Dennis and cadging smokes.

Up on the shaky scaffolding next to The Thunder, Dennis could see the mountains too. All the years he'd been in Alberta, he never thought for a moment that he'd ever get tired of looking at the mountains. All around him, the plastic sheeting rattled in the gusty spring wind. He sat on the scaffold platform with his back to the plastic, absently counting the rusting and broken bolts and globbing the paint on thick. He figured that if he put it on heavily enough, it would take that much longer for the rust to bleed through. He'd been painting for days already, and figured he had at least another week's work ahead of him.

"Fresh paint can cover a multitude of zins," Mr. Reinhoudt told Dennis, his face serious, one pudgy forefinger pointed upwards. Remembering the words made Dennis smile; not all the words, he thought, only one. It was listening to the way Reinhoudt slowed right down and pronounced every single syllable of "mul-ti-tude," as if he was making three careful words out of one.

Dennis knew Reinhoudt was right—paint certainly could cover sins, at least as far as the provincial inspectors were concerned. Reinhoudt had told him that, and after a few years Dennis knew it was true. The rides really only had to look like everything was safe. Painting The Thunder meant that no one but him would even climb up and see if the supporting spans were still bolted firmly in place. There would be check marks in every single box on the ride's inspection sheet. The inspectors could have done their job just as well sitting in the front seats of their government pickups.

After The Thunder was painted, Dennis would be stripping the electrical circuits and brushes on the bumper cars and making sure all the loudspeaker wiring was okay. He had been at the park for twelve years now, and those were always the last few things to be done before the opening. The last few things, including replacing any of the hundreds of light bulbs that might have burned out or broken over the winter.

After that, it was just regular maintenance and lubing with the big grease gun, and a steady watch on anything that looked as if it might be wearing out. He was the eyes and ears of McNally's Fair. If the screech of metal on metal in a ride sounded wrong, it would bring him up solid in his tracks. He knew every inch of the park, every hint of springs and cogs that had reached their point of protest, with only days to go before total failure. He knew it, Dennis thought, like an ulcer patient knows the protesting sounds of his own stomach.

Last, of course, was cleaning up. Cleaning up. Dennis got a sour look on his face, even though he was high above the park grounds. His was a narrow, brown, sharp face but with piercing blue eyes like a husky dog's. Too spare to be handsome, his face always carried an expression of having something else in mind, some other plan. He looked faintly desiccated, as if his skin had dried out too much on some occasion and never properly recovered. Thirty-nine years old, with the bowling-ball beginnings of a beer gut, Dennis wasn't the sort of person even Reinhoudt would think of hiring now. But he was a steady, hard worker, and Reinhoudt had no trouble with the idea of leaving the whole park in Dennis's care for the six months or so when it was closed down, when Dennis lived there all alone.

Dennis had appeared at McNally's Fair in his truck, alone, the passenger seat piled high with full duffle bags and empty takeout coffee cups, the sides of the truck filthy with highway dirt. There was a flat spare tire lying on its rim in the box behind the cab, and Dennis's left arm was burnt bright red from the sun. While Dennis was talking to Reinhoudt, the truck ticked along gently as it cooled, standing high on its tires as if expecting to be told it was time to leave.

It was good timing for Dennis: Reinhoudt had just lost his handyman. Instead of two weeks' notice, the previous occupant of the job had simply driven away, giving the Dutchman the finger out the open driver's window.

"Don't expect your last week's pay," Reinhoudt had shouted as the man's truck started to pull away. The answer was short and sharp and started with "Fuck," Reinhoudt said.

Dennis told the Dutchman that he had experience with small engine repair and auto body work, that he had his own tools, and that he could start right away. Reinhoudt gave Dennis a quick up-and-down glance, his eyes staying on Dennis's battered hands and cracked nails for a moment, and then told him he could have a job. His first duties would be grubbing out the trailer where the last handyman had lived, and after that, Reinhoudt said, Dennis could set up in there as well—although it would be forty dollars a week off his cheque for rent.

For the next four weeks, Dennis barely spoke a word. Reinhoudt told him what needed to be done, and Dennis listened carefully, intently, as if he were listening to more than the other man's words. It was as if he were learning to listen to the entire place, trying to find out just what language the machines and people spoke when they weren't talking. Not speaking, Dennis knew, also gave him a kind of invisibility; he knew about that before heading out to Alberta, had known it for years. If you're careful and spend a month or two lurking on the edges of everyone's vision, he realized, one day they look at you and think you've always been there.

One thing Dennis didn't know was that it was a kind of silence often taken for disdain—and that it had coloured both his layoffs and firings in the past, marking him as the easiest one to let go when changes had to be made. The one who wouldn't complain, the one whose leaving the other employees would accept, the mood of the place brightening up as soon as Dennis and his tool box were gone. Dennis never said anything to anyone after the inevitable dismissal, even when he felt he had been singled out unfairly.

He had left the east coast when there wasn't any more work, when it felt like he had used up every possible job in the small Newfoundland town of Renews, a town where he had spent his entire life, in among a cluster of stubborn square houses around the horseshoe foot of a bay. He left behind a small bungalow on the black-rocked and often raucous ocean, and a quiet wife who was always in motion, always moving to another room.

His wife's name was Heather. They were the last ones in their high school class to pair up, and when they did, it had seemed to be because they both looked around at the same time and realized there weren't any other reasonable choices left. Besides Heather, Dennis could have picked Leanne Meadus, who lived with her grandparents and spoke so little that half the graduating class thought she was mute. Or Mary Wherry, perpetually the butt of jokes about her name until finally she tried, and failed, to get everyone to call her by her middle name instead. Heather could have chosen either one of the Power brothers, but she would have had to pick a time when one of them wasn't in jail for bootlegging or its intimate companions, high-speed drunk driving and fleeing from the police.

Dennis and Heather had simply waited too long to pick. It had worked for a while. They had managed an uneasy familiarity that felt a little bit like love, as long as neither of them looked backwards very hard at what their original expectations might have been.

They had managed to hold on to that pretence even after he moved away. For the first few years in Alberta, he would make his way back for the winters, once the park closed down, after his boss filled out the end-of-season paperwork and the unemployment cheques started. When Dennis was home, he and Heather managed to tolerate each other. But they moved in separate circles and only happened to intersect at their edges—usually the sharper ones. It seemed as if time apart allowed them to spend more time inside their own fortifications, walled into personal worlds where they felt safe and unexposed. Both of them might have said that the weeks they spent together felt strangely like surrender, as if they had let down the gates to an invading army.

At first, the cheques went one way and occasional letters came back. Four years in, a letter came that said he just shouldn't bother anymore. Dennis wasn't even sure that he minded. He thought he should mind, thought it should be obvious, thought he was meant to be broken-hearted, like the country music warbling out of the radio speaker while he was working or driving aimlessly on empty back roads.

Sometimes, he would turn around and be absolutely convinced that something was missing, as if he had lost his wallet or misplaced a false front tooth, but he couldn't put his finger on what it was that was gone. It didn't have a shape or a colour; it wasn't like a sweater missing from a closet, or an important tool left out in the snow overnight and buried.

Dennis couldn't imagine that it was as simple as loneliness, because he didn't think he was lonely. Nights alone at the fair when the snow was battering down had their own sort of magic, especially when he could come out of the trailer into the bitter sharp cold and feel the ice crystals finger his face. He woke up most mornings knowing exactly where he was, the rough grey blanket up around his chin and the sheets pilled with constant use, his eyes traversing the same water-stained ceiling without ever wishing that he was somewhere else, a feeling that he took as meaning he was close to that thing called home.

In the middle of the winter, Dennis would head out into the night and turn on all the lights in the park, forcing open the big guillotine switches with both hands, turning on the floodlights, and then, when the air was clear and cold and dry, he'd start The Thunder and take a few circuits all by himself. The grease would be stiff under the wheels of the cars then, and the wind would be like ice against his skin. He would hold on and make the circuits fast, wondering if the ride would shake apart from the unexpected winter travel, and at the end his hands would be as cold as wax. Then, when the ride stopped, he'd climb out and start it on its circuit again, leaping into the cars at the back as the front of the short train started up the track. It rode harder in the winter than at any other time of year: every corner struck harder, the springs on the cars yielded far less than they should, more punishment than pleasure. Everything was pushed to extremes, so the sounds he heard meant nothing. He would enjoy the rush and plunge of it, ignoring the angry sounds of the metal.

The lights looked best in snow, he thought, especially when the snow was fine icy shards and as thin as fog, and sometimes he would flick all the lights on in the park just for a moment, a blink of an eye, to see the brake lights flick on behind cars on the highway, the snowy spume lighting up red as each driver slowed for the multicoloured wonder of McNally's Fair, fading into an afterimage against the black of night. Times like that, he thought, it would be marvellous to have someone next to him in the front of the roller coaster, even if neither of them said anything, so that the sense of it could exist with someone else.

It was, he thought, a very small universe: the machines, covered and hunkered down in the snow, the boarded-up concession stands, the empty parking lot. But it was his universe, and he batted around through it in whatever order he liked, barely making his way outside the park's winter-draped fencing once or twice a week. For each one of those winter months, it was as if he owned the fair and every scrap of land it sat on, as if Reinhoudt barely existed.

He might not see anyone for as long as a month, except when he made short trips out of the park for gas or groceries. With groceries, he used to make small talk with the clerk at the FastFood, whose name tag said she was April. She had jet-black shiny hair and a curious way of holding her mouth when she wasn't talking that was almost like a self-conscious and constant sneer.

One night, he even made an awkward try at talking to her—at least, he was pretty sure it was awkward.

"Pretty girl like you gotta have a boyfriend," he said. She stared at him impassively as she bagged the groceries, never letting her eyes fall from his face, while he reddened and wished the bags would fill more quickly.

A week or so later, she accepted an offer to go to a movie with him, smiling slightly and looking off to his left as she gave him directions. He wondered if she was the kind of girl who would smile goofily and feel her breath slip away on the roller coaster, or whether her lip would just stay curled the way it was in the store, as if her mouth had been formed and left to harden awkwardly.

But when the snow came and boxed him in again on the night they were supposed to go in to Calgary, Dennis didn't mind. Instead, he spent the night circling the park and leaving trenched trails behind him in the shin-deep snow, carefully tying down every loose and flapping piece of tarpaulin.

When he went back for another load of groceries a week or two later, neither April nor Dennis mentioned the movie date they'd missed, and Dennis stared out through the big front window without looking at April as she filled the bags, as if they'd both come to the conclusion that the idea had been a bad one they'd agreed to forget about.

Once the grip of the prairie winter let go, his horizons expanded beyond the narrow trails he beat through the dry snow—trails he would often have to break out every single morning after the night wind had filled them in. When the snow rotted and shrank—faster where the wind had mixed in dark stains of fugitive soil—Dennis would watch his world expand with every single day of melt.

He had his pickup and the mobile home at the back of the park, and his hours were pretty much his own. Once the day was finished, he could pile into the truck and head into Calgary if he liked, or go out on the dusty roads through the farmland and scrub. He could head through the reserves towards the mountains, or just park his truck near the highway where the huge drifts of grey rock were thrown like tongues licking out from the fast mountain brooks that disappeared as soon as summer really arrived.

As it got drier, Dennis imagined that the dust trails behind the truck stood out like arrows, highlighting the roads behind and pointing directly at him, so that anyone who cared to look might find him at the very apex of the cloudy triangle, racing away frantically like a shiny armoured beetle. The drier the summer roads got, the higher the dust rose—and the more work there was to be done as rides ran full out and their parts wore out and failed, to the point that it seemed it might never end. The dustier it got, the more deceptive the prairie became, as if it too might never really end, as if each turn and twist simply led to more turns, each straight line to its own unreachable vanishing point.

Driving back to the park, there would just be the prairie, starting its gradual roll towards the foothills, and next, the top of The Thunder would rise over the hilltops, and the park would suddenly be there, poking up out of the ground like some unlikely industrial island. On more than one summer evening, he'd been at the top of The Thunder, doing the inspection and watching how, just before twilight, the prairie looked for a moment as if it had all turned to water, shimmering in the weakening light. It made McNally's Fair seem even more like an island, he thought, or maybe, now that the roller coaster was half painted, like a ship, with the huge sheets of plastic flapping in the wind like untended sails.

From high in the scaffolding, brush hanging over the paint can, Dennis saw Michaela coming out of the family's trailer. Something about the girl had changed over the winter, he thought. She'd always been pretty, but now Dennis couldn't help but watch the woman as she headed for the office, unaware of his stare.

Michaela was Reinhoudt's only child. Reinhoudt told Dennis he had been hoping for a boy, and that they'd already had a name picked out: Michael. Never one to waste anything, Reinhoudt had added an *a*.

Every summer, the Reinhoudts brought Michaela with them. She'd stay in the city with relatives until the school year was over, and then she'd appear at the park, filling different jobs: taking tickets, then working the canteen, her forearms specked with small scars from dropping the french-fry baskets into the hot grease. When she started taking commerce at university, she took over the big wooden desk in the office trailer, doing the accounts for the whole operation.

The woman now in the office was a big change from the angry teenager who had sat in the front of The Thunder on one of Dennis's late night test drives because they were sharing a smoke, the red coal at its tip bright from the wind, when Reinhoudt trundled into view below them. She'd muttered "Shit!" urgently under her breath, ducking down out of sight, and Dennis could still remember the heat of her breath that night, warm and damp against the outside of his elbow. She was angry a lot then, especially with her father, and Dennis used to keep her cigarettes for her and listen when she trashed her father for everything from his strict rules to his disdain for any boy who came to pick her up for a high school dance.

Dennis could see the silver roof of the administration trailer from the scaffolding, and he imagined that he could look right through the flat metal. He knew the office well enough; he picked his pay up from Michaela every Thursday, and he even had a key to the trailer in the off-season, so that he could get into the filing cabinet for purchase orders when he needed spare parts. There was a slatted swivel chair in the office, and he could imagine Michaela in there, head down and looking at papers. He couldn't decide whether her legs were stretched out under the desk and crossed at the ankles or if she sat with one leg drawn up underneath her. The thought nagged at him a little as he worked, as if he had a picture almost completely drawn up but some critical part was still smudged and unfinished. He could draw up everything else in his head: the big farming equipment calendar that Reinhoudt received every year—a mailing-list mistake, with a label that always read "McNally's Farm," but Reinhoudt wouldn't return it because it was free; the piles of invoices; and a big oily pin that had sheared off the main linkage in the Ferris wheel, which Reinhoudt was trying to get the manufacturer to take responsibility for.

But he could picture Michaela best of all.

She had a narrow, thoughtful face, and it seemed to Dennis that it was always turned down, so that she seemed to be looking somewhere close to your right bicep—a slow, curving smile and dark, peaked eyebrows. Reinhoudt was florid and blond, with a wide, flat, expressive face. Often, Dennis couldn't finish a sentence without knowing exactly what his boss's response was going to be. Michaela's mother's name was Anna, but the woman was so mousy and quiet that Dennis could hardly imagine she had anything to do with her daughter's features; it was as if even her genes had been too shy to contribute.

He thought about Michaela a lot while he worked on the scaffolding. He thought about what her world must be like, about how soft her long dark hair must be. Sometimes, about how a towel must feel against her skin when she was getting out of the shower, but he always tried to shake that thought out of his head.

It was cruel to bring a young woman like Michaela out here where she was stuck almost all by herself, Dennis thought, looking down at the Reinhoudts' travel trailer. The trailer came out from Calgary at the end of April. Dennis heard they had a big house in one of the newer Calgary suburbs, one with a fancy name like Tuscany or The Hamptons. He'd never seen it. Hard to imagine giving that up to rough it in a travel trailer five months of the year, Dennis thought, and he'd said as much to Reinhoudt. Reinhoudt told him, "You don't run a good business from fifty miles away."

The words had stopped Dennis in his tracks. He'd been halfway towards saying, "That's not the only thing you don't do from fifty miles away." And for a moment he'd remembered his wife's face, but then it was gone.

Unlucky in love, that's how Dennis started thinking about himself, remembering his last sexual encounter, a front-seat blow job on a dirt road near Regina from a hitchhiker he'd picked up as he raced across the flatlands, wondering when they would ever end. She'd briefly replaced the empty coffee cups in the front seat and was, he thought, someone who had picked him simply because there wasn't anyone else in the truck to pick, and he wondered if that didn't actually match the run of the rest of his life.

The summer after Heather told him not to bother coming back, he spent a lot of time driving, often stopping to watch when a freight train came thumping along the rails next to the road, counting the cars and reading the different railroad names on their sides. Pulling over when he saw small hawks cutting shrinking circles in the sky. Eventually, what had seemed like home out east came to feel more like a healed fracture than anything else. Sometimes, when the weather changed, he would feel a deep, twinging pain for a little while. But there was always Aspirin in the cabinet in the bathroom and rye in the kitchen cabinet with the plates, and it didn't take much to shove it all away, once he had dinner in front of him and the television on.

Finally, the high first arc of The Thunder was completely painted, the scaffolding all moved to the next curve, and Dennis suddenly took Michaela in his arms as she came out the office. As he did, the lights all started coming on, and he could picture short, portly Reinhoudt at the heavy switches, bracing his feet and grunting, pushing up.

Dennis wrapped his arms around Michaela, reaching all the way around the slim woman's back so that he could hold on to his own elbows behind her, just after the sun had swollen up huge and had bent down into the clouds on the horizon. Just a quick hug was all, he thought, and she was so thin and soft and quiet there in his arms. He'd had a few shots of rye up on the scaffold, and it had started to make sense in his head. He'd known her for years, and she'd always been nice to him, made him feel as if he actually belonged there. And now it was as if she belonged here, notched in against him, like they fit together. The quick, copper-mouthed daring of it, like taking a chance working alone on the top of the roller coaster's first arc, no safety harness, only trust in balance.

"We could go out," he whispered into her hair. "We could go into Calgary, maybe dancing. Catch a movie in town. Maybe just drive around out here to where we could see the stars better."

But she broke out of his embrace, her face frantic, as if she was frightened. He felt suddenly guilty and looked at his hands as if they belonged to someone else, and he remembered how smooth the side of her face was against his own, how pale her skin was compared to his own burnt arms.

Once she had pushed him away, she squared her shoulders and looked at him.

"Look," she said, and then stopped.

And he knew she was Reinhoudt through and through after all. Her father had exactly the same way of throwing out single words as if they were meant to define everything—one word that set the scene and made the rules for everything that was to follow.

"Look, Dennis. I don't know what you're thinking, but I'll tell you this." And then her chin came up and her eyes were coal-black under the brightening arc lights staring down onto them from above. "You've worked for Da for a long time, so I'm not going to say anything to him about this. But I'm not going out with you—I'm not going to Calgary with you, not going in the truck with you. Not if you were the last guy on the planet. It's just not going to happen." While she was talking, she was stepping backwards, and sliding her hands one after the other down her arms towards the opposite wrist, as if she were wiping off something unpleasant that had gathered on the fine hair of her forearms.

At least, that was the way it seemed to Dennis—and even as she kept talking, he couldn't shake the image from his mind. He knew she was still talking, but the words seemed to be missing his ears. Then she stopped and turned, striding away, leaving a brightly lit Dennis standing at the centre of the park.

One of the big sodium lights blew then with a dull thump, throwing a circle of dark all around him, and in his head, Dennis was already going to get the big ladder and a spare bulb, wrapped in its nest of corrugated cardboard. You have to be careful with the big bulbs, he knew. A touch in the wrong place and you could immediately mark the new bulb for failure: the small whorls of oil from just one fingerprint could make the quartz glass heat unevenly and crack. It said so right on the box. One errant touch and you'd ruined everything, you'd have to start all over again. Dennis headed towards the shed where the ladder was kept, and he could hear Reinhoudt nearby, swearing loudly; although the big bulbs lasted for ages, they were, according to Reinhoudt, unreasonably expensive.

Dennis looked up towards the horizon, towards the big, bright green arc of The Thunder, standing like some kind of rigid, unripened rainbow. He knew it didn't matter how many times The Thunder was painted and repainted, every time he rode in one of the cars, he could tell by the sway how much more the cross-members sagged. It was drooping even faster this year, bolts stripping somewhere, the first turn bottoming out deeper than it should—and even fifty coats of paint couldn't disguise that from him. He'd talked to Reinhoudt about getting someone to come in and look the ride over, someone who actually knew what they were doing, but he could tell right away that Reinhoudt wouldn't do it. He'd gotten a dismissive wave. "It'll be running fine after I'm dead and gone," Reinhoudt said, almost shouting, "Nothin' wrong with The Thunder. Nothin' paint won't cure."

The next morning, Dennis went back to painting, and thinking about Michaela.

He put the brush down across the top of the paint can and looked at the palm of his hand, where the green paint had bled through the bristles and had run down the handle onto his skin.

Funny how different it could look, he thought, just funny, the way the green paint made the hairs and pores and wrinkles stand out that much more when you looked close. He stretched his arms up above his head, and looked out across the flat of the prairie. You couldn't see the new grass if you looked directly at the ground, he thought, but if you looked across the whole prairie and let your eyes go, you could see the green fuzz of spring coming.

So high up, Dennis thought. So high up and so far down.

911

*I*F THE ROOF LIGHTS hadn't been on, I might have gotten away with it.

I might have been able to wiggle my way out of it somehow.

I might have been able to explain that I was transporting a dead body because no one else was available, just trying to help, that the victim had run out of time. They might have listened to that.

Because they would have been happy to take any explanation. They were waiting for one, for anything, so they could get out the old rubber stamp and close the file.

The siren? Sure, lots of people might have heard it while I was going up the hill, but it really could have been anyone—a police car somewhere, or firemen late for dinner, heading back to the fire hall, slumped back in their seats and tired.

But the lights: accident investigators know about lights.

I know too, because I took the courses, back when I thought I might want to do something else—back before I knew that this was the only thing I'd ever want to do. Break a light when it's lit and tiny beads of glass will form on the filament, glass dust melting on superheated wire right before the filaments fail. Or something like that. The point is, the filament is different if the light breaks while it's lit, different from what it would be if the light was turned off. And you can see it as clear as a bell under a microscope, if you're looking. And they'd be looking—too many different stories to ignore impartial evidence.

I knew they'd have me with the lights, and it was only a matter of time. Besides, the police had to already know I'd been going fast from the way the rig was wrecked. You don't do that kind of damage tooling back to the hospital at fifty kilometres an hour.

But waiting for the reports gave me a window of opportunity. More to the point, it gave them a window of opportunity. When something goes really wrong, you always have that window. It was the window for me to quit or resign, to take away the need for them to do anything, so they could wash their hands of me before they even had to talk about the "organization's reputation" being damaged.

Problem is, I don't give a damn about the organization, about the hospital or anything. I just care about the job, and they know it.

I remember the thistles. That's the last clean, clear thing I do remember. I remember seeing them, and thinking I was in big trouble. They were on the side of the road on White Mountain. The ambulance was going wide open, and the headlights caught the thistles on the shoulder all at once, lighting them up flat so they only existed in two dimensions. Big and tall and completely covered in thorns, their flowers a sharp purple on their bulbous green tops. I saw them clearly, before I drove straight through into the big nothing behind them.

So that was me: Tim McCann, already suspended but still driving an ambulance at top speed right over the ditch and into an embankment on the other side. It was the kind of thing the media would feast on if they found out.

It was a big old TopKick ambulance, the kind that looks like a van with an extra foot of roof stacked on top. That's the extra headroom, so you can stand up and work back there. But they're pigs on the road—too high, the wheelbases too narrow, and especially tippy when it's slippery. They're like some kind of curious hybrid—made for a different job, made to make do. Underpowered, too, compared to the new box-backs.

There are always supposed to be two of you, two on every call—two to get the gurney back into the ambulance with the patient strapped down; one to stay with the patient, one to drive. You're not supposed to try to do it all alone. But I thought even me alone had to be better than no one at all.

See, I waited, listening to the radio, and no one was kicking out of any of the stations when they called.

There's a big round clock in the ready room at the ambulance station, up by the wall-mounted television. The ready room is full of battered institutional furniture, the kind you get when everyone sits on it and no one really gives a damn about coffee-cup circles or creases in the vinyl from too many asses for too many hours. The clock has black hands for hours and minutes and a slender red whisker for the seconds, and that red hand just went round and round, and the dispatcher kept calling different units, but there was no one answering. I wasn't even in uniform, no black pants or white shirt, but I was wearing the blue polyester zip-up jacket we all had, the kind of jacket that might get you a minute's attention from the girls behind the counter while you're belting back coffee and doughnuts in the middle of a quiet afternoon.

I was picking up the personal stuff from my locker that I wanted to hold on to until the suspension was over: five days, no pay, in trouble again because of my mouth, because I told an administrator, Pat Riley, that I didn't give a fuck about forms. Riley snapped back, "I'm trying to keep you from getting sued," and smart-mouth me, I'd said, "Hope you like your job. Mine is saving lives."

Too damn self-righteous for my own good—and it got right up his nose, too.

So I got five unexpected, unpaid days off, a case the union didn't even want to fight, and because of that, I was in the ready room stuffing a bag with dirty laundry when the radio started chirping.

We were already down a full crew—early vacation that someone had approved, probably Riley—and all hell was breaking loose on the radio.

It was the sort of thing that nobody wants to plan for. In Kentville, the ambulance was tied up with a car wreck. I'd heard them roll with the fire department when I got in, and they were probably struggling with big tools and heavy bleeding. New Minas was transporting a heart patient into Halifax—a bad call when we were already short—and to top it off, I knew the alternator had gone on the rig in Canning, and they couldn't get a gig out of it, couldn't even get it to turn over. They'd been complaining about that rig for weeks, and now it wasn't going to move.

The dispatcher was marching farther and farther away down the valley, looking for a free vehicle. She was as far away as Berwick before I couldn't take it anymore. I couldn't take it anymore because there was no one to roll, and up on White Mountain, someone had dropped the phone after calling for an ambulance, and the dispatcher could hear the ruckus in the background, someone screaming, "Bill, Bill, talk to me, Bill!" and there were snatches of the dispatcher trying to get someone to pick up the phone, little bits of that being broadcast over the radio too, whenever the dispatcher keyed up the microphone.

The ambulances all have numbers on the back, and we had the very first ones, so the numbers started at 001 and went up from there. We joked about it being James Bond's EMS, "double-oh-seven, licensed to kill." EMS, that's Emergency Medical Service, like an ambulance, except we're allowed to do something to help instead of just loading you up and driving as fast as we can go.

I didn't do the radio call-out, didn't let the dispatcher even know I was on the road. I turned the key, and when 003 started, I took it. We hadn't stripped it yet, so it had gear, but it had been taken out of service, parked and waiting for a brand new replacement box-back diesel ambulance that was going to be the new 003—a bigger engine in a heavier rig with more room to work in the back.

003 would have been my rig anyway, if I wasn't suspended and John, my regular partner, wasn't home burning off overtime because he didn't have anyone to roll with. We're not that deep. There aren't a bunch of call-ins with paramedic training sitting around waiting for me to get suspended, so when I got five days without pay, John got five with.

It was summertime, so he and Kate had probably spent the day at home filling the kiddie pool with water for the youngster or something. And now, with no duty in sight, he was probably kicked back with a beer. John talked about his family so much, I felt like I knew them. Kate didn't like the hours, the rotating shifts, the job itself; John didn't like the complaining. They were made for each other. I wondered which would end first, the job or the marriage. I was betting on the marriage, but then again, I'm not impartial. It's hard to find a partner you click with.

I had to come into the ready room late enough to avoid running into anyone I knew. When I was out the door and the automatic door opener was closing it behind me, my ambulance was an invisible rig.

Driving, I heard the dispatcher, still trying to find a crew. She sounded patient, but also a little frayed. It sounded like Anna, the new, pretty one with the small, careful mouth and straight blond hair. We'd gone on exactly one date, she and I, and from then on she was busy every single time I called her to ask for a repeat.

She was still looking for a rig. Berwick was out some-where and they couldn't roll—and it was too damned far anyway.

Might as well send an ambulance from Mars.

I reached behind the gearshift and flicked the lights and siren on when the dispatcher finally found an ambulance in Waterville, because she gave the crew the address and I picked it right out of the air—"Code Four Medical, 1027 White Mountain Road"—and I'd be in there and gone before they even got off the highway.

I put the pedal down and ran straight up the hill, up past Prospect Street and the new row of subdivision houses, up towards the hilltop park and a wide, shaky turn to the left on loose gravel.

If it had been daytime, I can tell you that you'd have to agree it was beautiful country: big patches of open ground, fenced for livestock or blocked with crops, and it just gives you the feeling that the soil's so rich you could grow any-thing at all, even shoes or fridges if you had the right kind of seeds. But if you were riding with me, you probably would have been more taken with the big rectangular wing mirror, watching the rooster tail of dust fling up into the sky behind us. Or else, like John, you'd be watching the road in front, hoping like hell a cow or a deer didn't stroll onto the road, holding on to the dashboard for dear life the way he does almost every time.

I like to drive fast, and I'm good. I got to White Mountain faster than any other driver would have.

When you see a house with the front door wide open, it often tells you that you've found the right place.

I slung the ambulance around and put it right up next to the house, reversing up the driveway and nipping in across the grass because it would make it easier for me to load the victim if I couldn't get any help. Put the back doors almost to the steps, feeling the heavy ambulance settling down into the grass and soil.

Inside, it was absolute pandemonium.

I had hardly gotten in through the door when a guy grabbed me by the shirt and hauled me the rest of the way through, yelling, "What the fuck took you so long?" and I could feel spit spattering across my face in a fine spray. I had the trauma kit, and I sort of shrugged by the guy, pulling back away from him while moving forwards against the side of the hall. Angles are important for emergency work, like they are for a boxer. You give them an edge of you, like a bullfighter feinting, so they don't get a good grip and you can get by, like you were greased or something, because they get revved up and they're hanging on to you, not seeing how they're getting in the way.

There was a couple next to the sofa, and the television was on, and God help me, there was popcorn all over the place, all over the floor and the sofa and the chairs, like Orville Redenbacher had fucking exploded and the guy on the ground had been caught in the crossfire somehow.

He had it all going on. He was coding, his heart stopped, and I was cutting his shirt off and yelling "What's his name, what's his name?" because sometimes, if nothing else, that shuts everyone up.

The woman rocked back on her heels away from him, that kind of "I-can't-watch-but-I-have-to" thing, before saying, "It's Bill. It's my husband. His name is Bill."

Big bare-bellied Bill, pleased to meet you, I thought, and I was beginning to wonder if I'd ever get a call where someone having a heart attack wasn't just plain huge. They say people are getting bigger, bad diet and a lack of exercise, and I believe it. Often, we end up calling for another crew if we have time, because we don't want to end up injured too. Load some dying monster on a backboard and tear up your own back trying to lift him? No thanks. People make their own beds; sometimes they die in them.

This looked like the rush didn't matter. Bill was bluish on the sides of his face, lips like blackberry juice, and I figured I'd be going through the motions, more for everyone else's benefit than his. And fuck me if I didn't stick the HeartStart defibrillator patches on his big naked chest and give him one quick jolt, and damned if the thing didn't actually start him right back up again.

What a moment that is. I'm not religious, not a bit, but I swear, it's just like having God right there in the room when they go from nothing to a heartbeat. It's not something you get to see very often: zap a slab of already-dead meat and then see it open its eyes and blink at you, like it was a guy asleep in bed and you'd woken him up with a whopping great electric alarm clock or something. Especially when it's been forever since you hit the road in the first place, and by all rights he should be stone cold dead by now. The only thing I could think was that he'd collapsed, but his heart must have kept ticking until just before I got there. Because sure as anything, that heart was stopped; it doesn't matter how big you are, if you've got a pulse, I'll find it.

That changed everything. Now, instead of transporting what I was sure was going to be a body, I had to get Bill to the hospital. And quick.

I yelled at the guy who'd grabbed me coming in, got him to go out and wrestle the stretcher out of the ambulance, and we rolled Bill up on one side and down onto it and cinched the straps down.

"Aren't there supposed to be two of you?" the man asked after we got Bill into the back of the rig. I deliberately ignored the question.

"Tell his wife I'll meet you guys there, Eastern Kings Memorial," I said, because Bill needed to be stabilized at the closest hospital before anything else, and I slammed the double doors on him, my last look inside the ambulance seeing Bill's big tented feet under the sheets.

I ripped the rig out and down the driveway, cutting the wheels hard and feeling the back tires tearing up the grass. I put the siren back on again, and the lights.

Then I got the shock of my life from the back of the rig. Because Bill was talking to me. Honest.

For at least a mile, Bill was talking to me. I turned the siren off then, still driving fast. He told me that he'd been watching hockey and that someone had scored—he couldn't even remember which team was playing—and the next thing he knew, he was out on the floor. He was getting it out in short sentences, breathless, a few words at a time, as if he was feeling the shape of each individual one of them in his mouth, like hard candies.

Then I was walking through all the heart attack symptoms with him—crushing pain in the arm, shortness of breath—and he had them all. But he was lucky: he had been stopped and then started again. On any medications? "Insulin diabetic." Any allergies? "Cats—but I hate 'em anyway."

I swear, once in the conversation he even laughed, telling me he had heard his wife scolding him while he was lying there, that she was sitting there yelling at him for dying. I remember thinking right then, the ambulance roaring bright through the night, that this might actually work, that I might get him there in time. I remember also, at virtually the same instant, thinking, "Don't even think it," because you might not believe this, but in EMS we're the most superstitious people alive. When we walk back to the station with a coffee, we'll hop, skip and jump to miss every crack in the pavement. We'll stop to pick up lucky pennies. We'll count crows, "One for sorrow, two for joy," and if we see just one crow, we'll stop dead until we're sure we can find another, even if we have to pretend that a green garbage bag caught in a tree is really a bird.

There's enough working against you already. All you
need is to jinx it, all you need is to make it a little bit worse.
You take every single bit of luck you can get, and still lots of
people die before you even get close to the hospital.

Then, from the back of the rig, I heard a short, hacking
breath.

"Thanks, bud."

It was breathy and thin, and it was the last thing Bill said.

Then I heard a grunting sigh that sounded like it was rattling right up from his stomach, a big sort of gurgled breath,
and I knew it was bad. I knew that sound, and if I had been
working with John, I know what kind of glance would have
gone between the two of us. It's a bad sound.

"Bill?" I called towards the back of the ambulance, my
eyes still on the road, the lights cycling off the trees in bright
red and white splashes as we flicked by. "Bill?"

Nothing.

And if they've coded, if their heart has really stopped
again, you've realistically got four minutes on the road before
their brain starts to burn out. Every cell in their body crying
out for oxygen, and not finding it, because the blood's not
trucking it around anymore.

I did the math. I couldn't stop to check, not by myself,
because it would take too much time, even if I managed to
shock him again and get everything going. Bill had been
gone once already, and the odds just weren't in my favour.

So I started screaming.

I was screaming "Talk to me!" through the walkway back
to Bill, and I was screaming down the road from White Rock

too, my foot right to the floor, the ambulance shaking wildly on the dirt road, and I could hear that everything in the back was coming apart.

I knew exactly where I was—up over the top of the ridge now and heading down the hill towards Wolfville—and I thought hard and decided that I might be able to make it. Four minutes, and if I drove fast enough, if I didn't get stopped anywhere, I really could be there in under three. I had the siren back on again by then, and the engine in the TopKick was going flat out.

Everything in the back of the ambulance is held behind Plexiglas sliding doors—blood pressure cuffs, pressure dressings, IV bags full of sterile saline—and the faster I went, and the more potholes I hit, the more things were raining down on silent Bill in the back. It would be like a ticker-tape parade of medical gear back there by the time I got to the hospital, but if I got there in time, who would care?

The rig felt like it was in the midst of shaking apart, like the wheels were going to fly off or I was going to break an axle or something. There are rules for how fast we're allowed to go. You might not believe it when you see an ambulance ripping up behind you in the rear-view mirror, leaning out to change lanes and moving so fast that it tilts, so fast that, in your car, you can feel your body cringing, waiting for the speeding rig to clip the side of your car, but there are rules about how you drive. I'd pretty much broken all the rules anyway, so I had 003 wide open, the engine roaring in under the hood, not another vehicle in sight out in front of me.

I was calling over my shoulder again to Bill when I piled hard into a big pothole I didn't see in time, and the whole front end of the TopKick sagged. It sagged, leaned to the right, and then the headlights didn't even line up properly anymore. The steering wheel didn't seem to be attached to the wheels. And I saw thistles, a crisp, even green line of them, just for a moment. Thistles, like a line of exclamation points, the punctuation at the end of a sentence, a run, a career.

They told me Bill was dead before we crashed.

"All of the injuries on his body were post-mortem." That's what the final report said, and that's coroner talk to take home with you to rub on your conscience like ointment, because it's supposed to mean, "You didn't kill him."

The stripe of the strap cuts below his shoulders, even the gash over his eyebrow where the monitor unit had come off its brackets and hit him, the crushed bone where his ankles had been—none of them had bled at all, not even a little seepage, meaning his heart had completely, absolutely stopped before we crashed.

The ambulance went straight down into a ditch, the front right tire blown out, with me high up over the steering wheel so that I cracked four ribs and smacked my temple when we hit the embankment on the other side. And the whole TopKick must have almost stood right up on its nose then, everything inside flying apart, before landing on its roof and crushing the light bar.

The ambulance from Waterville found us, rattling their way back down the hill from a house where they'd been told an ambulance had already left, and they had no idea who it might have been. They found us because the headlights stayed on, and they said I was still unconscious when they got there. It's a wonder I remember any of it.

My partner John came to the hospital—Kate waiting with the kid in the car—and he was still on days with pay, a free vacation. He told me that the ambulance had held together all right, that even completely upside down the clamps hadn't let go of the gurney wheels, and Bill had been hanging from the ceiling like a stranded parachutist when they had forced their way into the back, the back doors crushed up and into his legs.

John looked at his hands when he talked. "You're in shit this time, Tim," he said. "You're surely in shit this time."

He kept looking at his hands, scratching at the rough patches, pulling off a fragment of fingernail. "Any one of us, we would have done the same thing," he said, but the words sounded wrong, as if he was suggesting they wouldn't have done quite the same thing, really.

No one from any of the other crews came in to see me. The union sent me a fruit basket, but I didn't even take the Cellophane off it.

I might as well have been infectious.

So, do they fire me because I was out on the call alone, because I didn't wait for a duty crew to finally make their way up there? Or will it be because I wrecked an ambulance with a patient strapped into the back? The insurance company was certainly going to raise hell, because I was suspended and driving an out-of-service rig. Just about the only people who weren't mad at me were Bill's family. They even sent a card.

I'm going to get canned now, I remember thinking, just because I couldn't help but do my job. You'd think I'd be the kind of guy they'd be desperate to keep. I've had three sick days in five years, I've taken every scrap of overtime they've ever asked me to take, and I've got a whole year's vacation banked because there didn't seem to be any point in taking it.

When Bill's wife came in to visit me, I didn't recognize her. She had to tell me who she was. Away from that house, away from the scene, she didn't look like anyone I'd ever met before.

"You did your best," she said. "Sometimes that's all you can do."

I shook my head, told her I was sorry. But I didn't tell her that it was our fault, that we should have had more rigs on the road. That maybe her husband wouldn't have died.

She stayed by my bed for a while, while I thought about what I hadn't said, and what it all meant.

And I'd be stupid if I didn't know what was coming next.

Riley's expecting to give me a lecture and a chance to get out clean, a chance for me to quit and save him a raft of problems. Riley's waiting to tell me that I rode a full wagon into the ditch and someone died as a result. Riley's a vicious bastard; he might lean in real close and whisper, "I've got you this time, fucker," when my union rep's picked up my file and turned away towards the door.

But I don't think so. Because Bill's wife is sitting by my bed, and I know exactly what I can tell her, and exactly what the ambulance system doesn't want her to know.

Lying there, I had a message for our precious administrator.

I want my goddamn rig back. I'll trade him the vacation and the sick days if he wants, offer them up to burn off a suspension if he wants.

But I want my rig and my partner and my goddamn job.

And he's going to give it to me, too.

Because if he tries to hang me out to dry, I'll hang him too.

Not enough rigs on the road. Not enough of us to work in the shit and the blood and the rest of it, the siren rippling past the thistles and through the black night, the rig all lit up and heading for another bad surprise.

If I have to tear the whole place down around me, damn it, they're going to have to put me back out there.

FAMILY LAW

ENNEBURY versus Hennebury was up on my computer screen. It was Nova Scotia case law, and I wasn't really sure it would apply here, but I read it anyway, trying to see if there was anything worth keeping, even hidden between the lines. I wanted to collect all the pieces, to try to see if there was any way they might fit into the case I was working on, to see if they had a slightly different take. Looking for something I could toss up in front of the judge, as much to confuse as anything else. Give them more detail to chew over. More for them to think about.

Applicant and respondent were married for twenty-three years, two children, one of the kids already in college. The judge calls them the husband and the wife all the way through the decision, even though it's basically the last official time that anyone will ever call them that.

Hennebury is fighting with Hennebury over pensions, the pair of them having finally settled the child and spousal support in mediation, but the whole case is now breaking on the shoals that he has registered retirement savings plans and that, while she does too, hers are considerably smaller.

I took notes, marvelling as I sometimes do that my hand-writing can be so small and round and even, so preciously trained into my hand, despite the turmoil that's overtaking everything else I do.

The judge, who was named Doyle, reduced the entire case to spare prose and straight lines. I envy that kind of simplicity: simple language and obvious, basic logic, no stopping for broken dishes, revenge and recriminations. No late night crying silenced with fists pressed up to your mouth so the children don't get woken up. No vicious words that smack into each other and hurt, words that you no longer even have the will to try to undo. Just huge amounts of two intertwined lives reduced to mathematics: this share of the matrimonial home set off against that share of the summer place and the car.

There was bitter late March sleet coming in over the harbour in St. John's, straight off the ocean and completely unforgiving, and it was catching like a solid orange curtain in the lights over the pier where the offshore supply boats dock.

It was eight-thirty, and I was still in my Duckworth Street law office, staring through the big square windows out into the night. The office is in a three-storey green clapboard building that I and my partners bought and renovated. We rented out the ground floor to a souvenir store, so sometimes in the daytime when there's a quiet moment I can hear the bells they have hanging over the door to let them know when customers come in.

Down on the street, everyone had been reduced to the oversized black wet footprints they left behind after they'd gone. It was a hopeless kind of night, a frustrated, nasty kind of storm, a leftover scrap of winter that should have already given up but wouldn't take no for an answer.

There were cases I should've been working on, scattered across my desk in buff file folders with multicoloured tabs, and hours full of work that was supposed to be billed out to clients. Instead, after endless Internet searches of marriages gone wrong, I found myself sitting at my desk, occasionally balling up scraps of paper and throwing them across the room into the wastepaper bin, wondering just how I ever got into this business.

And why I stay in it.

Well, the why part—actually, I know that. There's an explanation right out front on a brass plaque by the front door: *Williams, Carter and Wright, Family Law*. Williams and Wright have gone home, along with everyone else in the office. We do well on other people's misery; the money's good for partners, even in a town with a clear oversupply of lawyers. I'm the Carter in the middle of the sign. Michael Carter, twenty years out of law school now, forty-seven years old and greying at the temples in a way I tell myself is distinguished.

I've been a lawyer long enough that I keep expecting to see my name pop up on the Queen's Counsel list, for longevity and constancy in political donations, if for nothing else. I'm fit enough for squash, handsome enough for deliberate flirting, and old enough to regularly be brutally practical and hate myself for it. To make my way straight to the point and to get rid of all the non-essentials right away.

It wasn't always that way.

In law school, I was well steeped in the idea that everybody deserves representation in a necessarily adversarial system; that everyone needs an advocate. That's the kind of word they always used in law school, and it sounded grand the first time I heard it. I suppose for journalists it must be the "freedom of the press" kind of thing that resonates, just the way that for doctors it's the Hippocratic oath.

But eventually, you get used to the comfort that good money brings, and that begins to ring true more clearly than abstract principles. So you keep on going even after you start doubting.

I expected to leave law school and stand up for people who couldn't stand up for themselves. I always thought I'd be there to give them the kind of representation they needed, when they were too busted up to do anything. Except that it all grinds you down; it all works away at you like the ocean chewing away at the edge of a cliff. Family law is forty percent—no, more like sixty percent—about someone else's disaster, and there's hardly ever a client who doesn't start crying in your office at one time or another.

Sure, they thank you sincerely enough when everything turns out all right, even though nothing ever turns out exactly right. It's no wonder divorce lawyers generate so much hatred. Too much of the job is trying to balance distinctly different positions against one another, and the compromises always cut someone. Often, they cut everyone.

And it's amazing how many cry even when you win. Some of them never manage to stop.

In Métier versus Métier, in the New Brunswick Court of Queen's Bench, the wife wanted to take the children halfway across the country to Alberta because she had a boyfriend there with a good job. Her ex wanted to stay where he'd always lived, in Bathurst up on the North Shore along the Baie des Chaleurs, even though he was on unemployment half the year. A judge named Simon had to decide whether the once Mrs. Métier could follow love and make a new life for herself, or whether she had to answer to simple parental fairness first, staying somewhere where all the personal wreckage would be visible outside her front door every single day.

Often the judge takes the easy out, and says that something or other would hurt the children—and almost always, when the kids come into the equation, when they turn up in the judgment, it means the status quo, the staying put, will win. When I hear the word "children" come up when I'm in court, listening to a judge reading a decision, I know right away where the chips are going to fall, even though I always wonder who the hell really knows what's going to do the most damage to kids.

In Barrett versus Barrett, Ontario Court of Appeal, the husband wanted a cut in support payments even though he hadn't ever bothered to pay anything. Ever. And the wife wanted every missing payment back to the dawn of time. The total her lawyer had worked up at the bottom of his submission looked like the kind of number you usually associate with a lottery win. That's a case where you can tell that someone—probably everyone—is bound to end up dissatisfied.

There was a French case I once saw where everyone was accusing everyone else of spousal violence, and the kids told the judge they didn't want to live full-time with either parent. The husband said the wife tried to run him over with the car, and the wife said she had her right hand slammed in a door. I can imagine the daughters, three little girls, lined up prim and proper and serious in pressed dresses in front of the judge. Their names in the court documents were a simple triptych—*A*, *B* and *C*—and in his ruling, the judge made each one of the girls out to be more mature than anyone else in the courtroom. And he was probably right.

Mary had left before the sleet started, when it was still fat drops of rain weeping down on the outside of the big streetside windows. I could tell that it was getting colder outside. The chemistry of weather was changing right in front of my eyes, so when the drips started to form into a lacy skein of wet ice at the bottom of the glass, I wasn't really surprised.

I watched her go, watched her heading down to the underground car park half a block away where the firm leases a handful of spaces. I never have to scrape the car windows when I leave work, but the route to almost anywhere is an uphill right-hand turn that's slippery whenever there's a snowstorm or ice.

Mary had the collar of her long coat pulled up around her neck and ears, and when she pushed her way into the rain, she pulled her head down into her coat so that it looked as if her neck had completely disappeared. I found myself hoping that she was warm enough, that she wasn't going to get soaking wet before she got down the short hill to her car.

I always think of Mary the way I know her best, eight buttons down on a smooth blue blouse, her arms always open.

While she'd been here, we'd left the blinds open the whole time, even though there's a hotel across the street with at least twenty rooms where anyone could just walk to the window and peer across into my office. You get to a point where there's a grim kind of fatalism to it all, where you know the end result is that you're going to get caught, and the only real questions are when and where and how. Because nothing except being caught will ever be able to break the spell.

Mary would be known as the *adulteress* if she cropped up in Smith versus Smith-Coté—Smith-Coté's lawyer obviously favours the classic language, and I expected a "heretofore" to pop up at any moment—and Mary, some version of Mary, appeared in her supporting role as mistress in Harris versus Pender, and Tobin versus Tobin, and Henry versus Barber-Henry too.

I used to get in trouble with clients sometimes, because they would say I had barely included the other woman when I was drawing up the nuts and bolts of their case, dismissing her in too few words, because she mattered, often passionately, to everyone involved. My problem was that, before Mary, I wanted to point out the far from surprising fact that a third party wasn't that original, that a sudden extra was always the protagonist in someone else's two-act play, entering right before the climax and staying onstage all the way through the short sharp slide to the denouement. But that, as much as she mattered to everyone involved, she didn't matter a bit to the law anymore.

It wasn't that simple in my own life, where the other woman was Mary. Suddenly it wasn't the way I'd always told my clients it would be—especially the women—the way I'd told them the other woman was just a transition, that she was only a bit player, and not to focus on her because the root causes of a marital collapse were sunk far deeper than whoever had recently arrived, the real roots were deep in the wreckage of a marriage they had already lost.

But with Mary, it was right and natural, the way things are supposed to be. And believe me, I know exactly how stupid that sounds. I've probably heard the same thing a hundred times myself from clients.

Sometimes, when everyone else is winding up for the day, Mary comes in to help me finish up the paperwork. I've spent the tattered edge of a hundred days watching my partners leave the office purposefully looking straight ahead and away, waving their good-night waves without even looking at us. Williams and Wright are perfectly happy convincing themselves they haven't seen anything if it's something they don't want to see.

Mary has been working with me for six years and she knows just about everything there is to know about me: my shirt size, my shoe size, the way I love to touch the wispy hair on the back of her neck. Yes, Mary knows way too much. She knows when my wife's birthday is, and twice she's bought Beth's birthday present because I was tied up late in court.

Mary knows both my kids, Will and Liz, and sometimes they've sat at her desk for hours while I finished up with a client, Liz with her tongue stuck out and a pen looking over-sized in her small hand. Mary's got some of her drawings up on the side of a filing cabinet, stuck there with tape because Liz gave them to her. William always wants to talk to Mary—always wants to talk to anyone, actually—his words the pure little ringing bell that is a young boy's voice. I wonder about the jumble of emotions she must feel every time she looks at those kids.

"Christ, Michael," Mary has said to me more than once. "I can't go on like this. It's ripping me apart."

She's right. And I can't either.

This is plain exquisite and unstoppable hell.

I know there are people who can go cold turkey, can decide to go back and try to rebuild the house that has crashed down all around them. I don't know how they do it. I don't know how they surrender what they've got, or how they could possibly go back, knowing that the marriage they're going back to will be even worse than the despair they were already in. That it will be every bad thing it was, along with extra servings of guilt and blame. You look at the ceiling in a house with a leaking roof and you always see the patches where the plaster is shot from water coming in, never notic-ing the parts where there's no mark at all.

In Matheson versus Matheson, there were no children, but there was twenty-eight years of combined property—includ-ing the matrimonial home and a cottage and an RV—and still, with all those years of water under the bridge, one of the two had made a list of every single wedding present, and whose side of the family each one came from. The judge bravely marched through the list, step by step, in his decision—red wineglasses to this party, white wine to the other—until he got to an entire set of copper-bottomed pots that he suggested should stay together, even if the marriage couldn't.

So, who gets the good memories, and the memories of the meals cooked in those damned pots? Who gets the inside jokes, now hollow because no one's left who understands them anyway?

In Royal versus Moore, they were fighting over the fact that they each brought condos and prior lives into the merged equation, and unravelling the tangle was as complicated as calculus—percentages and mortgages and different rates of interest, all being spun together into a knot while the judge hunted for fairness like an Italian hog hunting for truffles it can't see but still scents.

Every single case reduced me to almost complete, thudding despair, wave after wave of hopelessness passing over me and leaving me behind in the trough, followed by the next case that picked me up and flung me farther ashore. I couldn't stop reading, scrolling down through the legal websites and picking off every single case where two people with the same name were battling each other. Sometimes I got lucky and it was a probate case instead, a brother and sister fighting about some obscure or unclear clause in a will, and it was a relief to be able to follow the skeleton of the argument without having to invest anything in it except professional legal curiosity.

There was nothing pleasant or tidy about where I was, no legal shorthand that was going to make it all right. There was no excuse or even a clear explanation—and I wasn't offering or expecting one. It just was, and it had been from the very moment I realized something was wrong.

Mary had a familiar, sad half smile when she left my office, and she trailed a finger along the line of my jaw from my ear to my chin, cool, smooth skin, and she adjusted her clothes briefly before she left, like she was shaking herself into them, a motion that, to me, has a curious formality—and a curious finality—about it every single time I see it.

You're supposed to step back every now and then in my job. I kept trying to remind myself of that: step back to cut through the emotion and the fury and find the analytical lines that I used to use to make rational decisions—the sharp lines that clear points are based on.

Clients always want to explain what happened, and I always have to keep myself from stepping right in and stopping them. Why stop? Because like any lawyer anywhere, I bill by the hour, whether the discussion is useful to the case or not. It's like clients feel they have to regale me with the reasons first; that it's essential we spend a bunch of time on "she didn't care about me anymore" or "he picked up some tramp" before we do anything else. The whys don't matter to me, I've always wanted to say, and the hows matter even less. So let's cut to the chase and get the one thing done that almost everyone can agree on.

There was a time in divorce law when everything was essential, when blame was paramount and critical, when scarlet letters actually left a mark, but that's an archaic concept now.

People always want to put an explanation out there for why it all failed, for why they won't get to be the couple putting the fiftieth wedding anniversary advertisement in the newspaper, both of them staring out of the photograph like slightly amused survivors of a long infantry campaign. You always see the ones who made fifty; there's no newspaper ad for "crashed and burned two years in."

People don't want to hear that the successes are as arbitrary and chance-ridden as the failures, and that the reasons are only justifications for much more deeply hidden flaws. Even if reasons mattered in law, I'd have to tell them that I won't ever believe it was that simple anyway. I would never accept it was all one person's fault, no matter how egregious or horrible his or her behaviour. I'd like to tell clients we should spend the time in my office concentrating on what comes next, on where they're going, and not waste any more time worrying about how they got here.

There was a time when Beth and I spent every moment together. Joined at the hip, her friends used to say. It's trite, but every couple has to have those moments tucked somewhere into their joint past; otherwise, they wouldn't end up being couples, would they? No matter how hard things get later, those wonders, those high points, shine and prickle with possibility. If you never had candlelit dinners and firelight and fine-fingered passion, you would have found yourself shaking hands at the end of that first evening and looking forward to a date with someone new.

I can remember when Beth and I drove out to Bonavista, almost broke and making believe it was a vacation. We stayed in a small, square, flat-roofed white house surrounded by a patchwork green yard with boulders sticking up through it, close enough to the lighthouse that we could see the sweep of the light pass over us, peeking around the heavy curtains to finger into the room with every midnight sweep.

Occasionally, we even made our way out of the small house, and the owner of the bed and breakfast asked if we were newlyweds, and told me that we should eat well to keep our strength up. When I told Beth what he said, she had to hold a pillow over her mouth because she was laughing so hard. I can remember that the RCMP highway patrol was, for some reason, billeted in another room in the same Bonavista house, and they were always coming in the front door late and waking us up at strange hours so we could dive into each other's arms all over again.

I told Beth I kept expecting the cops to bust into our room, guns drawn, because they'd heard a struggle, which made her laugh more.

She used to laugh a lot then.

That was when we could park the car anywhere on that spine of Bonavista road and just walk out into the bog and brush, and never be at a loss for words, finding wonder right there in the juniper ground in front of us. We could walk for miles along grey stone beaches, hearing—almost feeling— the clatter of the stones pulling back into the surf, and never even have to speak. Back then, I could read a book about a couple being one and believe that I knew exactly what was meant. And back then, when we drove anywhere, no matter who was driving, the driver would reach across without even looking and put their hand either onto a leg or into the passenger's hand, the perfect marksmanship of familiar touch almost every time.

You keep remembering all that once it's gone, as if it's some kind of magic elixir you can draw strength from, strength you need through the times when you're not getting any sleep, through sick kids and colic and the whirl of endless turmoil in extended families. Things rush along, and you end up living a kind of dismissive shorthand with each other—no one to blame, everyone to blame. Because there's no time, and you forget to make time.

Until the day I woke up and realized that even the light outside had changed some time ago, and I suddenly believed that all the books had been lying about love, that it wasn't really endless and perfect and available after all. I also realized that I'd actually known this for a while, although I couldn't pick out the exact day when I'd discovered it.

It was like when autumn comes, when there's still sunlight but it doesn't have the same kind of warmth on your skin anymore.

I knew everything had changed.

When I asked her, it was something Beth knew too—except she told me she had other things to worry about, more important things, that she was overwhelmed by everything else in her world. She also basically told me, in just so many words, that I could deal with that loss on my own.

For weeks afterwards, looking out the windows of my office, my mind was in neutral, doing nothing to help except spinning around endlessly over the same knot, and cutting into my billable hours to boot. I was marking time, shifted away from any kind of action by the realization of the thing I had lost.

Oh, and did I mention how much Mary understands loss? Two kids of her own, two girls almost grown now, a single parent hop-skipping around the city enough that she understands real estate better than the firm that does our title searching, so that sometimes I let her handle the few realty transactions we do get, and I just initial them in the end. For her and the kids, she told me, moving was almost like painting; you have to do it right away when you realize that the serious marks are beginning to show through. She told me quietly that she's spent a life walking into relationships full of hope, and every time, she's either walked away or been walked away from. That it's hurt every single time, but in the end has always wound up being the right thing to do.

So she recognizes loss when she sees it, recognizes it like it's a fine new colour rising up under your skin, a nascent bruise.

And when it happened, it was just one moment, one single tipping moment, one switch tripped, one light touch. I can remember it absolutely exactly: her touch, electric and fine, like static chattering across my skin, drawn out over a full minute. After that, things simply fell into place.

In Markland versus Markland, a British case, the husband and wife shared ownership of a chicken plant, except a trust held the two deciding shares. The wife had told the judge that the trust was a sham, that her husband had always been able to coerce the trustees into doing exactly what he wanted, and the judge spent thirty-seven pages of his decision detailing what a *sham* is in law, and how it has to work. I believe the judge was actually just trying to delay the inevitable, that he had to make a decision one way or the other—that he'd already made the decision—and that he wanted to be saved from blame by deliberately burying himself in unnecessary and extraneous detail.

Reading the decision, I couldn't help but think it would have been better for everyone involved if he'd simply gone ahead and said it, instead of endlessly trying to straddle both worlds. On page thirty-eight, already easily twenty pages too late for everyone else, he finally said there was no proof to the wife's charges. But it still took another one hundred and twelve pages to finally finish the case.

In Traves versus Traves, Ontario Superior Court, there were no good guys at all, and the judge obviously held everyone, lawyers included, in complete disdain. Her verdict was full of sharp, angular words, chastising the husband for deliberately hiding assets and underplaying his vast income, lecturing the wife for theatrically overplaying her misery, and smacking all the lawyers for resorting to legal tricks and sharp practice. I got the feeling that if it was her choice, she'd have given all the property and cash, every darned bit of it, to charity instead of letting any one of that shabby crew benefit from it. There was disdain dripping from every judicial word.

But she analytically split the property up piece by piece anyway, the houses and cars and loans and registered retirement savings plans, and in her last paragraph she said that she had been as fair as possible in trying circumstances, where everyone had cheated in one way or another. Then the judge said she had absolutely no expectation that the case would end with her, that she expected everyone would appeal, and in the end their entire savings would be devoured by bitterness and legal fees.

And good luck to them both.

It read as if she put the last period on the page with a hammer.

It was completely unprofessional, and it was the sweetest judicial verdict I have ever read.

It was almost midnight, and the office was lit hard against the night. Shaken by the dark glass of the windows, I turned off as many lights as I could, leaving only the small circle of the desk light and the blue pool from the computer monitor.

With the light almost gone, the office started to take a shape from its sounds: the distant whirr of a motor, probably the refrigerator in the small kitchenette, and the occasional flat ping of the fins on the radiator when the heat came on. Sometimes a disembodied and regular ticking, something cooling down or heating up.

Outside, the snow had started battering down even harder, and the cars left trails that barely lasted, deep white-on-white indentations, the tires no longer cutting down to the black of pavement. The occasional passersby were crowned with white on their heads and shoulders, like small and moving mountaintops. Ranges coming into range, I thought, and the scrambled confusion of the words made me smile.

Down over the dock, I could see the coils of snow caught high and twisting in the orange arc lights, bending and running but, like moths, unable to escape from the glare they'd caught themselves in. Able only to lie down on the ground and die, exhausted by all the futile effort they'd expended.

I kept calling up more case law, tapping keys into the Ontario Superior Court and the British Columbia law library, sometimes taking a swing overseas through the European Union law archive for judgments that were at least written in a slightly different tone, different enough that I could almost hear the upper-class shape of the words. Reading family law reports from Australia and Scotland and New Zealand, soaking it all in, all the broken little pieces of glass that are right there, around the next corner.

As hard as I tried, I didn't find anything close to the simple answer I was looking for. Not anywhere.

Silvio versus Silvio. March, for some reason, versus May, like two different seasons at war: he's cold, she's blooming. Layton versus goddamn Layton.

Across the street in the hotel, a room suddenly burst to life, the curtains open, lights ablaze. There was a man and a woman, tight in each other's arms, and I could see them coiling against each other, urgent. I wondered who they were, if their personal and joined struggle—looking almost violent from this distance—was Married versus Married, or Lover and Lover.

Another time, eons ago, I might have actually joked that I could sit in my own office and drum up new business by the careful and regular examination of the rooms across the street. The couple in the hotel clearly didn't care about curtains, either, shucking themselves out of each other's clothes, and the irony was that I could watch without even getting aroused, keenly aware of what they were feeling and wondering if the weight of tragedy was just waiting to fall.

Whether or not I'd get to see it coming before it struck.

Whether I'd care.

When I was barely paying attention anymore, one of them turned off the lights and the windows went dark.

Ground down by the weight of a hundred cases or more, I knew that I would eventually have to stop reading, turn off the last of my office lights and lock the door. That I'd throw myself out into the night and hope that the snow would blast away everything from my skin and leave me shriven. Sandblasted clean. Home to a quick shower, the kept appearance of freshly painted and unmarked walls—and no questions, because questions have become a well-known, well-trodden minefield.

Magazines are always saying that there are a dozen signs your spouse is having an affair, and they're all true. What the magazines don't say is there's a point where you don't even want to know what the signs are, because it's the kind of addition that you just don't want to do. The sum is too definite.

All of the hotel rooms were either dark or had their curtains pulled closed when I turned off the computer and headed for the stairs.

I turned the key in the front door, felt the deadbolt snick into place, then pressed the familiar numbers on the keypad to make sure the security system was on. Out in the snow, I saw Billy Sharpe, crusted over with fallen snow like a statue. He's a process server, a guy who works for the firm regularly. When he moved out of the shadows, snow tumbling off him, the movement startled me. He must have rung the after-hours bell and somehow I'd missed it.

"Got nothing for you today, Billy," I told him.

"Well," he said quietly, and he shifted his weight and moved his hand into his pocket so the snow tumbled down over one shoulder in a brief and abrupt avalanche. That's why he's so good at his job—no one ever expects anything. He pulled out papers. "Actually, Mike, I've got something for you."

He said it apologetically, his eyes down at my feet, but he handed me the papers anyway and then moved off into the falling snow and out of sight so quickly it was hard to believe he'd even been there.

And I wondered what the rush was, wondered which lawyer in town was in such a hurry that they'd send Billy out in a snowstorm to wait up half the night for me.

I opened the envelope, unfolded the brief, and watched as the snowflakes fell down like little stars on the expensive paper, melting instantly and bringing the paper up in little damp humps like welts wherever they landed.

Looking at it over and over, I tried to make sense of the words while the rest of the world seemed to be grinding to a halt under the weight of the snow.

Carter versus Carter.

LITTLE WORLD

"MILLIE DOESN'T MIND if I come in, she never does. If she minded people coming in her house, she'd lock the door, wouldn't she? But she doesn't. She hasn't locked the door in years. Everyone knows everyone out here, we've grown up together, for God's sake. Right on top of each other, really."

Helen Goodyear was like a tour guide, explaining every single step.

"And you a police officer, it's not like you're here to rob anything."

Helen was a small woman, stooped, with an ordered pile of white hair. All of the knuckles on both hands were fat and angry red with arthritis, her face creased and brown from the sun. She was wearing a summer dress, blue, but the hem had come unstitched and she hadn't noticed, so that the skirt ended in an uneven fringe of ravelled cloth.

Helen stopped on the porch, turning as if the motion provided some essential piece of punctuation to what she was going to say next. "I tell you, I know what I saw. But I don't know if anyone else saw anything. You'll have to ask for yourself."

Behind the house, there was a big shrub rose, the white buds tipped with pink, falling over itself with the weight of the flowers that had already bloomed, the tips of some of the branches rubbing against the side of the house. Thrown over everything, the sound of the ocean, the swells running up the bay and falling on the stones, hauling the loose rocks back into the water with a clatter.

Helen stood in front of a two-storey house that had once been white, with rough-sided clapboard now showing through in patches. The peaked roof with its black shingles dipped along in the middle of the roofline in a gentle, hipped curve. Millie's house was prominent among the handful of houses in the bottom of the valley between the river and the road, the highest of the six in elevation, but the lawn was ragged and uncut, high with browning timothy grass, a spruce tree heavy in the front yard and the ground beneath it carpeted with cast-off needles and scattered wet spruce cones.

Millie's house was like all of them, turned so that it was facing away from the wind off the water. Each at its own subtle angle, backing or shouldering into the wind, not squared off like new houses on a suburban side street. The houses all standing as if they were performers in a play, caught fixed in time at one particular point in their blocking, each part of a lengthy and familiar conversation, lines practised and delivered over and over again. That was easiest to see from above: as the road curled in from Placentia, the houses suddenly appeared, laid out and clearly visible, so that finding them was like a discovery made while landing a small plane on a narrow asphalt runway.

"Millie's in here all the time, she's the best here for making bread, so I try to time coming over when there's bread baking, you can't beat that." Helen was talking so that her words were thrown back over her shoulder as she walked down the narrow hall.

She walked into the empty kitchen, put her hand on the cold enamelled stove that hunkered down next to the back wall, and then walked to the window, peering out through the small square panes of glass. The paint was peeling on the mullions between the panes, white once but freckled now with small black blemishes of mildew.

"She's not here, and I don't see her in the garden either, but she can't have gone far. Used to be it was like she was attached to her kitchen with string, she was that easy to find. For the last few months, though, she's never been here when I needed her. Maybe she's found a man." Helen laughed behind her hand at her own joke, her eyes flitting back and forth, looking for someone else to join in. "Found a man? She's the same age as me, officer."

Helen in front of the window, checking her reflection in the glass, tucking away loose strands of hair behind one ear. An old mirror, with the silver backing coming away in the corners.

"You can see all of the houses from here, we're always right on top of each other, everyone minding each other's business. You get used to it." She pointed outside, her index finger bent. Her hand was shaking slightly. "That's Wakeham's over there, he's a nasty old man, spits all the time, and a mouth on him like a sewer. Never anything good to say about anyone. And then, next to that, the two Hodges, Davey in the yellow house and Mike and his wife in the red one. My house you know, and the Slips are in that pale green one. They used to have two cars, in that narrow little driveway—can you imagine? And whoever was going out first took whatever car was closest to the road. Keys on a hook in the kitchen right inside the door, I could have taken one for a spin if I wanted to, and I don't even drive." She laughed, paused. "Not that I would, officer.

"Never see a car down there now. Must have taken them a little to get used to that. You can talk to all of them, if they're around. I don't know what they'll be able to tell you that I can't."

The house quiet, hot-air still, the rooms almost soaking up sound. There was only the faint ticking of the house shifting in the heat, individual boards giving a slight creak or an occasional snap as they settled, eased. No steady tread of someone walking upstairs—no sounds from outside. No shouts—no dogs barking.

The curtains hanging limp in the windows, exhausted.

"It's never really been a town. It seems too small to be a place that could have its own name. But it's been St. Peter's for so many years now, so I guess the highway signs are going to say that no matter how small it gets."

Helen opened the front door, revealing a rectangle of outdoors, the warmth of the summer morning flowing in through the gap like smoke.

The valley was cut up into rough squares with rail fences, the river fast and tea brown but low. The Slips' house with one broken window obvious on the second floor, a slight attempt at a repair with quarter-inch plywood. Down below, a lilac in the front yard, all of its blooms gone away, the branches heavy with green seed pods, the flutes of the blooms bleached and brown and scattered on the ground like intricately formed wet confetti. The small harbour a creation of time and the river's erosion. The belly of the valley full of dark soil and gravels pulled down from the higher ground over thousands of years.

Out over Placentia Bay, big clouds were scudding left to right, heavy enough to be thunderheads, waiting for just the right time to roll in like an army advancing and soak the land. Helen closed Millie's front door behind herself, looking around almost immediately, as if expecting Millie to change her mind and make an appearance after all.

"I'd take you down to see the Slips, because they're just as close to the water, almost next to the wharf, and their fishing shed is right next to the road there as well. But I don't think they're home. I don't see them much at all anymore, and without the cars, it's hard to know when they're there." Her voice suddenly quiet. "I'm not sure if they'd even come to the door. I think I may have done something to make them angry with me. It's not so very hard to do. If there's one thing they've always been good at, it's holding a grudge."

In the fresh air, the smell of the spruce trees on both sides of the river was stronger, as if the heat was pulling perfume out of the blue-green needles. The lupines were already dropping their flowers and setting seeds, the flowers that remained running up the side of the hill opposite like purple flames of a slow-travelling brush fire. There was one dry gravel road running straight down between the houses towards the bay and, springing from it like branches, narrow green paths that gave the impression of a community of sheep or other livestock, rather than people.

Helen was walking quickly once she reached the road, her feet kicking up dust and small stones, her voice echoing off the flat, square faces of the houses. "Before it was St. Peter's, it was just called The Green, and it was that for years and years. Even in a dry year when there's no rain for weeks and the hills go all brown, the valley stays green, see? The river gets low, but it never stops draining—and there are peat bogs up there for miles, just a big sponge sending water down to The Green all summer long. There's pasture here when everything else up and down the coast is dead and dry. But you know how it is: eventually a priest got posted down here on the shore who thought that saints' names were better. When it comes to religion, people are always willing to do what they're told."

Helen turning, stopping in her tracks, a small pale cloud of dust lifting up from her last few steps and blowing away on the light wind. "There have been people here for 180 years, you know. There used to be more people, sure, but 180 years? That's something. Fishing the whole time, when there were fish. Same families, same work."

At the last house before the beach, there were starlings nesting at the joint where the roof met the walls, tufts of sticks and straw visible around a hole in the clapboard facing. Occasionally, a sharp yellow beak and a black, glassy inspecting eye peered out, and then were pulled back out of sight almost immediately, like a curious neighbour pulling back a curtain. At one end the shingles were torn completely away, showing the boards of the roof, worn grey like the ribs of some large dead animal.

"My Patrick fished his whole life from here, out on the water almost every day all summer long, but for me it was a lot quieter. I'd wait for the boat to come back in, and when they were bigger, the boys went with him, until they moved away. Hard, steady work, and no money in it either. When there was fish, there was no price for it. When there was a price, there wasn't any fish. But you're not here to hear about that, I know. And we're almost there anyway."

The road curved slightly and ended at a concrete-deck wharf with yellow-painted four-by-fours all around the lip. There were tire marks on the rough concrete, from either a car pulling away fast or some sudden-braking game of ocean Truth or Dare. Helen stopped and pointed, her lips tightly pursed. "They came down right here, down to the wharf, just last Saturday. There's no boats here anymore, not full time, but that doesn't stop the government from coming down and fixing the wharf every year anyway.

"Kids come down here in the evening all the time in the summer, driving down from Placentia or St. Bride's, and you don't want to know the kinds of things they do in their cars. I mean, I'm sure you know, but you probably don't want to be seeing it right there in public any more than I do. One moment there's two people in the front seat, and then there's only one, and it's not hard for anyone to figure out the kinds of things that are going on."

A hard, quick frown crossed her face, disapproval cast in flesh. "And I pick up more bottles—liquor bottles, beer bottles, and cans too. Not out of the ordinary to have someone out there five nights or so out of the week when the weather's good, and sometimes you hear their music all over the valley—and believe me, it wouldn't be worth your while to go down and ask them to keep it down. Ask Millie about that if you get the chance—they'll say things you can't even imagine."

She stopped again. "Right here. That Saturday, they drove right out onto the wharf, the two of them, and he left the headlights on when he got out. It was eleven, but there was still a bit of light, no moon. And couples, you know, they fight sometimes, and they were just kids, really. They were arguing out at the end there, and until I got pretty close, I could really only see their legs in the lights. And she turned her back on him and he just put his hands in the small of her back and gave her a shove—just like this, just a little shove, but at the same time you could tell he meant to do it—and she kind of tripped over the edge and went in the water. And she came up angry, like it was a really bad joke or something, shrieking at him."

Helen stood beside the shed just before the wharf, showing how she had held herself flat against the side of the building and peered out around the corner, only a fraction of her face showing. In front of the shed, torn piles of net and a long rectangular pile of lobster pots, drying, dead sea urchins still clinging to the wooded frames and smelling like rot and iodine.

Helen looked down at the lobster traps. "He's not from here. He's from down the shore, but he works from this wharf for the lobster season. Used to be Patrick's fishing grounds before he died." She looked back towards the wharf. "Saturday, I wasn't far away, just here by the shed. Behind the shed so they couldn't see me, not that they were looking or anything, and it was dark anyway, and he bent over at first when she got on the ladder and climbed back up, like he was trying to help her out of the water, but then he just stood up straight and he kicked her. Kicked her right in the face, and she landed on her back, down in the water again, and it was like she was all loose. It was clear she was hurt."

Wind came down off the high ground then and wound close around Helen like an exhaled breath, bringing with it the smell of the ground juniper and the blueberries, the waxy richness of the rhodora. All around, things were moving, plants nodding, the new candles on the fir trees still fresh enough to flex up and down in the wind. On the horizon, the clouds continued their march, darkening.

"Then he got in the car and backed straight off the wharf, swung it around here where the road's wide and headed back for the highway," Helen said, and she was shaking her head while she said it. "I don't think he saw me, but the headlights caught in my eyes, and I couldn't see a thing then, couldn't tell you what kind of car it was or anything, not that I know that much about cars. And he was up the road and gone, just gone, tires spitting rocks back behind the car, and I couldn't even guess to tell you where he went after that, except that he turned towards St. Bride's, not Placentia.

"And I remember that as soon as the car was gone, I had the strangest feeling that I had gone deaf, as if after the noise of the tires squealing off the wharf I'd never be able to hear again. But then I realized that I could hear the waves. You forget about the waves—you hear them so much that you forget they're even there. But that's all I heard. I thought she might be shouting or something, but she wasn't. I know he hit her hard, the kind of thing when you almost feel it yourself, like your body knows what it would feel like.

"I went down to the end of the wharf and called out, but there was no sign of her, not a word or a shout or anything, and with the car gone, the water was as black as ink. I even went down along the beach, down there, because she would have drifted that way. There's a current right across the face of the wharf, and you have to watch it coming in and aim your bow as if you're trying to hit the right-hand side square on."

Helen pulled her shoulders back and shivered, as if the wind had turned cold and was coming in off the water. "I said to Millie we should call the RCMP right away, but she didn't say a word. I don't agree with that, but she has her own point of view. Always has. And we don't count on police much down here. We settle most things ourselves. Mike Slip and my husband disagreed about the bottom corner of our land, and things were bad for a few years, until they settled it themselves. But this is different."

Then back inside, the blue house this time, Helen's own house. "I've spent my entire married life in this house," she said, spreading her arms out as she said it. "My entire life. Patrick died here in the front room, and by the end I was exhausted from trying to help him breathe. I know it doesn't make any sense, but that's what you do: I would hear him rattling away down here, the cancer deep in his chest and him struggling, and it was like I timed every single one of my own breaths to be in line with his, as if I could help pull air into him. And he passed right here on the couch. It was summer then too, and the first thing that I heard was the birds, those little juncos out there, peeping. The only reason I could hear them was because I couldn't hear him anymore. He's in a grave up by Great Barrisway, his whole family up in there, and I suppose that's where they'll put me too, when my time comes."

The living room was small and close, a black cast iron stove squatting in the centre of the room, cold. "There was a time when that was the only heat, that and the oil stove in the kitchen, before we got the electric. I still have the oil stove— I just don't think the other stoves cook things as well. I haven't anything to offer on such short notice. I was hoping Millie would have some bread, you go over and she can't help but share, and I take advantage of that, I know I do."

Helen sitting down then on the couch, the small living room dark and smelling of damp. "He brought this couch in from the truck on his own back. He was strong like that, strong and stubborn too. You couldn't tell him anything. When we were first married, I thought I would change him, smooth him out a bit around the edges. But it always ran right off him like he wasn't paying attention at all. I had my own ideas, but a place can drag you down. 'Your own little world,' that's what Patrick used to say to me. 'You're just living in your own little world.' Millie isn't any better. Once, she said, 'You've got your head up there in a cloud, and I ain't saying a cloud of what.' And I suppose I did, making up in my own head the way things were supposed to be—that Patrick was a good man in a rough skin, heading out there every day. But it's important to keep that idea—it keeps you safe." She stared. "You've got to keep a piece of yourself there, you know. A shiny, safe little bit. Like a place you can go away into in your head."

Helen looked out through the curtains as if something moving on the other side of the glass had caught her attention. But nothing changed, the outdoors as still as a picture— each stalk of grass, each frond, suddenly still.

"That's something they don't teach you in any school. The trick is that you don't let go of that last little bit. That wary bit. You keep just a little piece of your guard up, if you're smart, just keep that little bit back inside you, and it will keep you safe.

"They don't do it now, you know, they're down on the wharf with their boyfriends and they don't stop to think that you always have to have a little part of yourself outside looking in. Just in case. You split something off to just keep watching. I've always been good at that.

"I remember I said something to Patrick once, it wasn't important, I can hardly think of what it was now, but he was moving logs in the stove, the little door open and the orange flames licking all around, and he had the poker in his hand, the short iron one, and the watching part of me saw his hand, just the way his fingers were around the handle, and all at once I knew. I knew because I was sensible enough to be watching, and really, I only had to take a couple of steps away—just enough space so he would think for a moment and change his mind before he actually got all the way over to me. You don't give all of yourself ever, that's for books, because you have to be ready. Have to know when to get out of reach, far enough away from the world that no one can touch you."

Helen's eyes were black then in the dark of the living room, her body perched on the edge of the couch like a bird about to take flight, her hands in her lap and busy with each other. The living room was cooler than outdoors, the air slightly thick with an unmoving humidity.

"You get better and better at it as you get older—put the walls up, and don't let anybody shift them.

"I thought I would find her the next day down by the rocks at the far end of the beach, but I didn't. That's where she should have been, unless the tide was strong and she got swept out around the point on that first night. I know I thought about finding her there where the beach goes away all to gravel, her hair spread out all around her head like a fan. I would have called you right away then."

Helen gave a brief, harsh snort. "Millie asked me if maybe I was making it all up in my head, she says I jump to conclusions sometimes, and beside, she hadn't heard anything. She claims a mouse couldn't come down the road without waking her up, she sleeps so lightly. But half the time when there are kids on the wharf she says she doesn't hear anything, and she's up above it all, anyway. Made me doubt myself enough to make me go down on the wharf to look at the tire tracks. I even got right down on my hands and knees and smelled them, just to see if they were fresh, but I couldn't tell.

"I'm sorry it's taken me so long to get to a phone and call you, but I don't think it would have made any difference. Millie probably wouldn't have called—I know she didn't want me to. She's a stupid woman, really, although I do love her dearly. She won't put things together even when they're right there in front of her face. She leaves things out to suit herself, and she just runs away when there's something she doesn't want to talk about. She says I live in my own world? It's nothing she doesn't do, but ten times worse."

Helen got back up from the couch, smoothing her dress down over her knees, looking around the room. "It wouldn't hurt for you to have one last look around the beach. I'll certainly walk down there with you, show you the top end where the current comes in close to shore. The place she should have wound up, all things considered."

Helen was quiet for a moment, then headed for the door. "Did you know my husband, officer? You look like my husband. He was from Great Barrisway. He was a handsome man, like you."

Helen looked around, blinking in the bright sunlight as she stepped off the porch and down the three sagging steps to the path. A pair of crows were calling back and forth across the valley, their ragged croaks hanging in the air.

"I don't know where Millie is—I don't have any idea where that woman might have got to. I suppose she'll talk to you. Maybe she won't. I don't think that she could have gone that far—she has to be around here somewhere."

She reached the beach, the great heaped stones of the barrisway, tons of rock brought in by the winter waves and thrown up in a long drift from one end of the cove to the other. Helen moved slowly, carefully, her feet slipping sideways on the round beach stones, heading for where the stones were smaller and the beach was flatter.

The black from the car tires, sharp-edged like ink on the concrete. The two black crows, high up in the valley, watching the woman as she walked. Helen completely alone.

NO HARM, NO FOUL

*L*ISTEN, I've never minded driving, and I've never minded company, either. I mean, if I don't have anyone riding with me, I'll even talk to myself, that's how much I like to have someone to talk to. Once, I was on that big wide toll road across Nova Scotia, heading for Prince Edward Island—that one that lets you miss the dangerous stuff at Folly Lake. I mean, there aren't any crossroads coming in, just trees as far as you can see, and most of them are tree-farmed black spruce, stretching out away from you in the straight lines they were all planted in—and I found myself answering my own questions, except I was answering them in a fake Scottish accent.

A guy in a big Crown Vic rolled by me, one wheel on the yellow and then the other way out next to the gravel on the other side, swinging back and forth like he's about to lose it all and roll into the ditch. Ten o'clock in the morning and he might have been loaded, for all I know. You see it all, you drive long enough.

And I said out loud, "Big car like that, and he has to be all over the road with it. He's not a very good driver, is he?"

"Nae, he isn't, laddie," I answered. "Don't ken how to merge or nowt."

All right, it sounds pretty stupid—and it was a pretty bad fake Scottish accent, too. But you've got to pass the time—and time, I've got a lot of that.

I've got a lot of all kinds of other things too. A lot of car, a lot of attitude, a big old sense of humour. A pretty big wallet back behind me. A fair amount of gut out there in front of me, too.

I sell. That's what I do. I've always sold, one way or another. They call me a "manufacturer's agent," but the truth is, what I'm really supposed to do is to get a product, any product, into someone's hands and make them think they absolutely have to have it. Right now, it's energy drinks—whatever the latest thing is, guarana, enough caffeine to straighten curly hair, you name it. Ten tablespoons of sugar hidden in a liquid thick enough to stand a spoon up in. In the past, it's been fruit juices, snack food, and once, for a while, even agricultural machinery. Agricultural machinery—I was a fish out of water with that stuff, even if I did manage to unload some once in a while. The money was good when you sold something—even three percent is a lot when you're selling something in the hundreds of thousands of dollars, just ask a realtor—but sales were few and far between. Ever buy a combine? Exactly.

Back in Halifax, I've got a little apartment in a big building full of neighbours I've never met, satellite television for company, and one goldfish who seems to be impossible to kill. I just give it as much of the food as I think it will take until I can get back again, and when I do get back, it always seems to have managed to stay alive. And if he—or she, I guess—dies, well, goldfish all look the same, and if you've given them all the name Fish anyway, they're pretty much interchangeable.

I hang the suit bag by the side door, back passenger side, enough clothes until I think I'll be back, and I take that into the motel with me every night, unless I want to advertise that I want someone to bash in my window and take whatever I've got. I bring the suitcase in and the samples too. Some people tell you they'd love to be travelling all the time, but a long time ago in a motel outside Corner Brook, Newfoundland, I spent most of the night listening to a bathroom tap dripping and had a little epiphany. There's a word for you. And here's what I mean: hotel rooms are all pretty much the same, just different places on a scale, and there isn't much you can call romance even in the good ones.

Maybe the good ones do stick in your memory for a bit, but the really bad ones do too—and there are more of the bad ones. I had a room near Amherst, N.S., that smelled like someone had thrown up in it. The carpet was soaked, like they'd run a faulty steam cleaner around the place that couldn't suck the water back up again, so I had to make a path from the bed to the bathroom with every single towel from the rack. There was another where I was right up over the bar, and when the band finally stopped and I got to sleep, the whistle blew for a four a.m. shift change at the paper mill. And too many times to count, there was a couple going at it in the room next door like it was some kind of Olympic event and they were damned if they weren't going to medal at least. Another place, none of the tiles in the bathroom seemed to be anchored to the floor, so that moving around the bathroom was like a stroll around a quarry.

But as long as the rooms are clean, I suppose I can live with it.

Driving eventually becomes the same too, regardless of how big your territory is; even new roads look just like the ones you're familiar with. I've got all four Atlantic provinces in my district now, from New Brunswick, where the roads are too narrow and too dangerous for my liking, to Nova Scotia, where urban is urban and rural can be, well, more than a little scary for the uninitiated. I saw a couple of guys near Kentville pushing a new bed home from a Stedmans store there once, just the two of them heading off into the distance, pushing a bed on those little metal casters for all they were worth. Stop to talk to them? Not likely.

Prince Edward Island? P.E.I. might be a great place for a summer vacation, but they're not so welcoming when it's winter and it seems that just by being there you're keeping some Islander from getting a job. I don't expect a lot of love in P.E.I., not in a big car with Nova Scotia plates. And Newfoundland? Sheer mathematics is against you from the start. A lot of ground to cover, not enough people, and not a lot of disposable income. Not much in the way of commissions to show for it. But it's part of my territory, and I'm expected to get out there, so I go through the island a couple of times a year, end up there for a month or so in summer if I can manage it, the same old familiar loops of highway over and over again.

And everywhere, I pick up hitchhikers. If I feel like it. If they look like people I'd like to talk to. Yeah, I know it's dangerous, but it really is better than talking to myself, no matter who I'm trying to sound like.

Once, outside Sussex, New Brunswick, it was a teenager in a long coat with a machete right up his sleeve. Couldn't even bend his elbow, his arm right out straight next to the door the whole time. I didn't see it until he got out of the car, so I guess he didn't think he needed to whip it out to protect himself from anything. But I saw it as soon as he closed the door, the blue-metal flash of the big curved tip. I dropped him near Saint John, in Hampton, I think, and afterwards I'm pretty sure we were both relieved.

Stopped for a woman on the side of the road in New Glasgow or Truro one summer. Whichever town it was, it was right above the Heather Hotel, anyway, you don't forget a place with a name like the Heather Hotel. And this woman—not young, either—she had her feet out of her shoes and up on the dash before I even got the car back in drive, and she was putting bright red nail polish on her toenails. Even had the little bits of cotton to stuff in between her toes, putting the enamel on as smooth and easy as you like, her in a little spaghetti-string top with these great tufts of hair coming out of her armpits like she was sprouting moss or something. The only thing I could think of was that I wished we were coming up on a bridge, so I could hit the seam in the pavement real hard and see if that would mess up her toenail-painting technique.

She told me she was going to British Columbia, that "life was easier there," but she didn't have much luggage and she must not have had much money either—offered to stay with me in my hotel room in Moncton, but I bought her dinner and begged off instead.

One of the worst? A guy I picked up almost next to my hotel in Bathurst, a big burly guy in a jean jacket who must have seen me loading my sample cases into the trunk, because he tried to rob me until I opened the trunk for him and he realized he'd just won a year's supply of high-octane sports drinks. More than a couple of those a day and he'd have been jitterbugging like a crazy thing around the back of whatever police car they finally put him into. I don't think he even realized he was a hitchhiker until he saw the suitcases going into the trunk—guys like him give the whole bunch of them a bad name.

And then there was Lisa. The worst one of all.

She was almost in the middle of the road when I saw her first, wearing just a T-shirt and jeans, and it was pounding down rain, halfway down the Salmonier Line about as far east as you can go on the Avalon Peninsula in Newfoundland. I'll tell you, May isn't always the friendliest month in that province, not even the last week of May when everyone else in my sales district has all the leaves out on the trees already. I was coming around a curve at the bottom of a long hill, coming around the curve fast the way you do when it's a little after seven-thirty on a dark spring morning, full of rain, and there's nothing else in sight. You watch for moose that hour of the day, not for chop-cut dyed pixies in soaking-wet Levi's.

And there she was, looking right at my car and waving her arms over her head in that frantic way that means anything from "Give me a lift to the store, would ya?" to "My parents' car is over the embankment and they're trapped down there."

So I stopped, and she came around to the driver's side window, a little slip of a thing like a drowned rat, and she struck her hip off the mirror, hard—I could see that in her face, the flash of pain, and then she put her left hand down and rubbed where she'd hit.

"I'm trying to get back to the cabin," she said.

"What cabin?"

"I don't know. The cabin. I haven't been out here before, so I'm not really sure. Can you give me a lift?"

There are cabins off the Salmonier line, alright, a fair number of them, and I can tell you just where the side roads go off, because I've driven by them more than a few times. I mean, even if you're on your own on the road all the time anyway, sometimes you like to turn off the main drag and see how the other half lives. You know, the ones with houses and families and cottages and Jet Skis and the cold beer on a big deck next to the barbecue. But there weren't cabins where she was, just a few miles above where the road goes across the Salmonier River. She was close to the gas station, and I looked in the mirror before I stopped and there was nothing back there behind me but empty, wet road.

It was pretty clear she was drunk, or at least had recently been drunk. There was a smell coming off her, a smell like plums or something, the smell that always lets you know someone's been drinking. I looked in the mirror again, hoping someone else would be coming, that maybe I could pass the buck, get moving and let her take her chances with the next car. It was still pretty dark, and the spruce trees come right down to the road there, so it all looked like something out of Little Red Riding Hood. I was just waiting to see the wolf, and meanwhile the girl was cold and wet enough that she had started to shiver.

"Come on," I said. "Let's see what we can do." And I reached across and unlocked the passenger door.

She walked around, and I watched as she trailed her hand, the tips of her fingers, along the edge of the hood as if her balance depended on the contact. She got in, fell into the front seat really, her hair all stringy and down around her face, soaking wet. I wondered for a moment about the seat, pushed the thought away, looked straight at her. She had a small face, framed in by her hair, a snub nose but pretty, and she was right on that age line where her face was changing into what it would look like for the rest of her life. That spot where you lock down the laugh lines or a permanent pout. Blue eyes that would be prettier if they managed to focus a little better.

"Paul Lambert," I said, and I stuck out my hand like we were being formally introduced somewhere. She just looked at it for a moment, like it was a fish she was trying really hard to focus on but wasn't really interested in touching, and then grabbed it.

"Lisa Rhodes."

I'll admit it's not the brightest thing I ever did, telling her my real name and everything. Or any of the rest of it—none of it was really bright. I know it's always easier looking backwards, when you can look at any one of those hundreds of spots where everything could be different, where you could have said, "Well, that's it, then, have a nice day," and you could just walk away, take a different turn.

But that's not the point.

"I've been walking on this damn road for hours, and it hasn't stopped raining once," she said. It looked like she was telling the truth: she was soaked through, enough so that I could see the lines of her bra under her shirt, and on both sides of the road all of the spruce trees were pulled downwards from the weight of the water on their branch tips.

"Where were you going, anyway?" I asked.

"I was up at the cabin, some friend of David's place. Over there." She waved her hand over her shoulder. "All guys. All drunk. You can imagine where that was going." She looked confused for a moment, as if she had lost her train of thought, and then her face cleared a bit. "So I started walking back to town. I think back to town."

"Town's an hour's drive," I said. "I don't know how far it would be walking."

"Whatever. I guess I thought they were supposed to come looking for me, right?" The girl was looking out the window as rain poured down the outside of the glass. "And maybe they were going to apologize for being such dicks."

With her inside the car and the windows rolled up, the smell of booze was much stronger. It was the kind of smell that would get you into the back seat of an RCMP cruiser for a date with the Breathalyzer, if a cop pulled you over for speeding or no turn signal or something.

She leaned against the window then, and it made it seem as though just reaching the front seat was the end of a long climb, and she was perfectly happy with staying put and thinking over how hard done by she was. Like she was more concerned about how it was everybody else's fault that she'd gotten into this jam than she was about how she was going to get out of where she was now.

Guys, you know—we like to jump right into problem solving. Even if no one's asked us to solve anything yet.

"I can't run you back into town—I've got places I've got to be this morning—but maybe you can go back to the cabin. Maybe they're all sleeping it off by now."

She didn't answer.

"Which way did you come from?"

"Don't know. It was dark. You're right—they should be sleeping by now. We were doing tequila shots at four and Dave had already passed out when I left. I just stumbled out and kept walking. I only found the highway 'cause a car went by and I saw the lights."

She would have needed those headlights. People who work all the time in the city, they don't really know about dark. Out on a highway without street lights, rain clouds covering the stars and any moon there might be, you're lucky if when you stop for a piss you can still find your zipper. I tried to picture her making her way along the road, one foot on the pavement, the other on the gravel, just to keep moving in a straight line. Lose your way just a bit in the black and the next thing you know, you're right in the middle of the road. I had my alternator go once, night driving on the highway just up from Gambo, and when the battery went dead, it was like I'd gone blind or something. I used my cellphone—not to call anyone, not way out there, but to use the light on the display to get my stuff out of the trunk and wait for a car to come along.

"Do you remember coming down a hill," I asked her carefully, "or did you just walk along the flat?"

"Down a hill, I think," she said, and then she smiled a bit for the first time. A little lopsided, but it sure brightened up her face. In a nice way.

"There are a couple of places—back at the Deer Park, or maybe the Colinet Road. Any of that sound familiar?"

"No. The cabin's brown, I think, and there's a white pickup out front. Dave's truck. Big truck."

I told her we could take a look, that I'd drive her back up the hill and we could see if she recognized the place. By then the rain was coming down in sheets again, and if anything, the sky was getting darker. Water was rushing downhill at us in the ruts on the pavement, and when we turned in the Deer Park, the trees were whipping around in the wind. We drove past a few cabins, then a few more, sometimes just driveways, and the puddles were hiding bigger and bigger potholes the farther back into the woods we got. I'd point to a place and she'd look, shake her head and rest the side of her face against the window—and every time, she seemed more and more resigned.

"I've only been there once," she said thickly. "If I see the truck, I'll know it."

"Are you sure you came downhill?"

"I think so. I dunno."

The air in the car was getting strong, and then the rain was slacking off again, so I opened the window and swung into a driveway to turn around. "We'll try down on the Colinet Road," I said, but she didn't answer. I thought for a moment she might have been sleeping.

After that, the conversation got a little bit strained. Well, her part of the conversation did. I kept talking, and every now and then she'd grunt or throw a word in somewhere. We had a twenty-minute drive or so in the other direction, and I told her about being on the road, about hotel rooms, the whole thing. How you meet lots of people but have to make your mind up about them really quickly, because you don't get to spend much time with them before you're gone again. And sometimes she'd rouse herself for a minute or two, enough once to tell me that she had finished school and had been working at everything from landscaping to home care, trying to find something that suited her. About her basement apartment, and how she wanted to get a car of her own.

I think I told her about ten times as much. Heck, I even told her about Fish, and then I told her I thought she was one of the ones that was all right, but by then she was really drifting—when she looked at me, it was like only one eye was focusing on me at all, the other one kind of drifting away as if it had lost the only line between boat and wharf. Not a pretty look for anyone. We passed more cabins, she shook her head, and we got to the end of the road and I got ready to turn around again, and I was beginning to wonder if I was ever going to get her out of the car. She hadn't seen anything familiar anywhere, not a landmark or a familiar sign or anything.

And then she was sound asleep.

She was right out of it, and with the car stopped to turn, I got my first real chance to have a look at her, curled up against the door with her two hands, palm to palm, tucked in under her cheek. And then I took my right hand and reached across and brushed the side of her face, her cheek, with the back of my hand. And I swear, she nuzzled over, moved towards me and smiled with her eyes still closed, smiled like she liked the feel of it, as if she liked being there, as if she even liked me. Somehow it seemed as though she belonged there in the car—and sure, she was only in her twenties or so, and I'm in my forties, so mathematically she could have been my kid, but you know, it's not impossible, you hear about it happening with other people and everything.

There's a little shift that happens, and it happens all the time, in all kinds of circumstances. Like your eyes suddenly are working a different way, and you size everything up differently. It's like when you make the sale and you sense it: even the air changes, and you know from their expressions

you could practically say, "Our drink is made with only the
finest crushed glass," and you know they'd go ahead and buy
it anyway.

That's the way I felt, looking at her. Like it was the difference between someone you've just met and someone you
know. Like I could know what she was thinking, and what
she wanted, and maybe it was me. A long shot, but maybe it
was me.

Don't get me wrong here. I mean, I know all about "no
means no" and I would never—but, I mean, she wasn't saying no.

She wasn't saying anything.

I just kept looking over at her when I started driving again,
at that little sort of half smile and the way her hair had dried
all feathery in around her face. We were just driving back up
the road by then, no point to it really, the cabins going by on
one side, and I knew that eventually I'd turn around and the
cabins would all be going by again on the other side.

Then I just turned the car up one of those narrow little
forestry roads, the ones where you push through a tight little
throat of spruce trees and then you pop out on a full-sized
logging road back along the edge of some clear-cut, green
just starting to come up between the wet-black stumps, and I
stopped and put the car up into park.

The rain had stopped completely, and we were up pretty
high, the front of the car pointing out over towards the river,
and mist was jumping up from the bottom of the valley.
Jumping up, rising fast, coming out from under the trees in
fast, reaching fingers.

It was an older clear-cut, the slash all knocked down by age, the sort of place where, even though it looks like a war zone, enough time has gone by that you know nature's going to take right over again, that it's just been biding its time until it's sure you're gone. Time can heal some pretty big wounds. Fireweed first and raspberries, then the quick deciduous trees like alders and impatient birch.

Lisa didn't wake up when I turned the engine off. I could hear her breathing, I could almost feel the long, deep breaths. Stertorous—that one's as big as *epiphany*, and every bit as precise. She was out of it, out cold, probably unconscious.

I got out of the car and looked down the long clear-cut into the valley. It's strange—we spend so much of our time around people, it's almost impossible to take in a big long sweep of trees and stumps where there's absolutely no people at all. No one in sight. No one who would hear anything. Some old, flattened cardboard beer boxes on the forest road, soaked through and coming apart, so there had been people recently, but not now. The air full of that smell of wet that you get after rain, the tinny sharp smell that makes you say, "Yeah, I remember that," just before you go ahead and forget about it all over again.

I remember hitching my pants up over my ass. I mean, with a gut like mine, I know I'm always hitching up my pants. They're always heading somewhere south, almost like they have a mind of their own, and they'd like to be somewhere warmer. Like Cuba. But I remember that time, that hitch, like it was some kind of punctuation, as if it meant something particular, as if it were a step forward the way a ratcheted gear turns—always forwards, never back.

Always done—never undone.

I went around to Lisa's side of the car and looked in through the glass at her, and it struck me that she was a far prettier girl asleep—that talking, or at least talking when she was drunk, made her face move in almost unattractive ways. I thought that, lying there asleep in the soft light coming through the mist, she was possibly as pretty as she would ever be in her entire life.

I opened her door, and she snored a little, but she didn't move, and I lifted her legs out through the door, her head sliding back against the side of my seat. She shifted a bit, but her eyes didn't open. Her mouth went slack, though, loose almost, and that was jarring.

I was picturing her just like that, exactly in that position, leaning back against the seat—but I was picturing her, after I'd taken her pants off, naked from the waist down and her legs spread and hanging out through the front door, the balls of her feet touching the ground.

I mean, I could have done it, could have done all kinds of things, and no one would have known a thing. Even if she woke up or something, even if she called the cops, just her word against mine, and me a working stiff with a clean record.

I could just say I didn't do it. Just like that: I didn't do it. Who would they believe?

Somehow, all at once, even imagining it, even fantasizing, it wasn't the way I thought it would be. It was like a crime scene photo on a television show. And in my head it was like someone had switched a light on for a moment, and just as quickly switched it off again. That spot where all the possibilities become impossible.

Worse—they became ridiculous.

I became ridiculous.

I don't like to think about that.

Nothing happened. I swear. Absolutely nothing happened. Anyone says anything different, they're lying.

I don't know why I feel like I have to keep saying it, but I do: nothing happened. I'd tell the police that if they asked me, and I'd try real hard to keep my face straight, because I always get nervous when I'm afraid someone thinks I might be lying.

I left her, wide-eyed and sitting on a swing set by the school down there in the valley by the river, looking for all the world like she was ten years old or something. She was awake by then and the rain had stopped completely, and she was pretty much dry again anyway. Lisa thanked me for trying to find the cabin, and said it was good of me to pick up a drunk stranger and let her sleep it off in my car. Good that a stranger would be willing to keep an eye on her.

I didn't say anything about that. I told her she should just wait, but that I had appointments down at least as far as St. Vincent's, maybe even Trepassey, and I'd keep an eye open for her when I was coming back up along the Salmonier Line, that if she was still there I'd give her a lift back into the city. Except I wasn't going to be looking, at least not in the way that meant I'd actually stop if I saw her.

After that, I kind of forgot about her for a while. I mean, there aren't a lot of stores on the way down, but there was a lot of fog, and the road winds right along the coast, so I guess I kind of slipped into the driving part, and then, in the stores, right into my patter about which energy drinks were best and how, if nothing else, they'd get the cleanest, highest margins on ours, a storefront display and prizes for customers who could be bothered to peer down inside empty cans to find a machine-written code.

By the time I headed back, six places had agreed to go on our distribution list, and that was a pretty good day for me, even if they never even managed to sell out their three-case introductory order.

Coming back by the school, I tried really hard not to look—I tried just to keep my eyes to the front, but it didn't work.

She wasn't there. At least, she wasn't there in the quick little glance I let myself have in the end, speeding by. No Lisa, no T-shirt, no high little firm ass in tight jeans. Stop it, I said to myself, just stop it. Stick with exactly where everything stopped: no harm, no foul.

I didn't really start worrying until I stopped for gas and the guy who owned the store said there'd been all kinds of racket, and he hated when someone went ahead and had a big May party. "Four o'clock in the morning, and some drunk girl is pounding on my door, loaded, and don't think I'm going to go out there to let her in. Pouring rain, and she was howling. But who needs the trouble?"

I told him I'd given her a ride, that she was only a tiny thing, maybe a hundred pounds soaking wet—and she was soaking wet, too. And how much trouble could she possibly be, anyway?

"I'd think twice before I did anything like that," he said, and he was shaking his head, putting the sandwiches and the water into the bag. "You're a guy alone in a car, and you picked her up?" He handed me my change. "These days I'd think twice about that for sure."

And that got me thinking.

I mean, if she got it into her head to say something about me, to say I'd done something, it's just my word against hers. It doesn't matter that I could tell them that nothing happened, not if she was saying that something did.

It would be even worse if I lost it and tried to lie about it, tried to say I hadn't seen her at all. You hear about the police using DNA evidence all the time in the papers, about how there's always a drift of particles, of skin and hair and cells, coming off us all the time—so even if I said I hadn't picked her up, there'd be plenty of proof that I had.

I can lie with the best of them about whether or not you need whatever I'm selling this time, but I'm not so good about lying to cops. Or to my mother. Or to anyone else who's willing to stare hard at my eyes and wonder why I won't look straight back at them and hold their gaze.

What if she didn't turn up somewhere afterwards? I mean, what if I dropped her off and something happened to her after that?

I know I keep coming back to this, but nothing happened up there on the forestry road. Nothing I haven't already said.

I know it just makes me sound more guilty to keep coming back to it. But I'm not guilty of anything but thinking.

You can't be prosecuted for the things that go through your head. It's only the things you do that are supposed to count.

After I got back to Halifax, I started thinking that maybe I'm not meant to be on the road anymore. Too many hotels, too much travel. One too many close calls. I know for sure that I'm not meant to be picking up hitchhikers. Maybe the smart thing to do, the next time they offer me some management thing, is to park the car for good and get used to a desk instead.

Buy a house. Meet someone. Get a real life.

Me and a goldfish and a wife. And smaller things to worry about when everyone else is sleeping.

LOOK AWAY

THE DISHES weren't done again, just piled up in the sink, crusted with dried food. I could see the ring of grease around the upper edge of the tilted plates where the sink had been left full until the water went cold.

I had pulled the plug out myself the night before, looking at my face in the black mirror of the night window, at the sharp silver-grey patches that had suddenly appeared in my hair at the temples. I thought that sometime in the morning the sink would get filled again with hot, soapy water and the dishes would be washed. But morning came and still they sat there, waiting.

Through the narrow gap of the half-opened bedroom door, I could see a wedge of green sheets, crumpled in heaps like big round-topped waves, the comforter down on the floor. The bed unmade again, thrown back, thrown apart, the sheets and blankets looking as if they had been discarded as unnecessary. That's the way she got up, the way she always had: just flinging the bedclothes back as if they weren't even there, padding away on bare feet to whatever morning errand she'd already set her mind to.

She might be anywhere in the house, caught up in a book or another important project, down in the basement or even outside.

Madeline doesn't care much about anything anymore, living inside her own schedules and plans, and the kids are every bit as bad. Half the time they're trying to hide from me, part of a petty little game I am far past appreciating, something that they keep doing over and over again, no matter how many times I've asked them—told them—to stop. Imagine a small boy hiding in the bottom of a closet, hands pressed across his mouth, trying to keep the laughter from leaking out, hiding while his father tries to find him and get him ready for school. Now imagine how irritating that is about the fortieth time in.

So I did the dishes myself, listening carefully enough to finally be sure they weren't somewhere in the house, wondering just where the hell they were this time.

The lightkeeper's house at Cape Pine is small, sure, but at least it's got electricity now and running water, so we have a washer and dryer, fridge and stove, and most of the time the dirt road's passable enough. It's tucked down in the bottom corner of Newfoundland's Avalon Peninsula, not quite far enough to the east for the kind of renown of a lighthouse like Cape Race, where ships used to cross the Atlantic just to pitch themselves ashore on the rocks, but it's important enough to be staffed, even though it's out of the way. In the wintertime we leave the car up near the St. Shott's road and go in and out by snow machine or on foot, but it's a far cry from the days when it must have been almost a day's hike to get out to even the smallest town, let alone a larger place like Trepassey.

I still remember when I got the registered letter telling me that I'd gotten the job. I'd be in charge of the Cape Pine light, a cog in the Coast Guard. Weeks would go by and I wouldn't hear from anyone, except for the regular direct-deposit statement that made its way to my post office box in Trepassey.

"Keith Pomeroy, Keeper" it said on the envelope, and Madeline and I both thought that was funny. For a while. Everything funny wears off with enough use.

Cape Pine is a big old lighthouse, built out of ancient stacking cast-iron rings, and it dates back to the 1850s, the metal heavy and rusty and always damp to the touch, able to grab moisture out of the driest air, and with its fog and mist and wind, Cape Pine is anything but dry. Sometimes it seemed like the old structure was weeping rusty tears: the heavy, glutinous paint would bubble out in fat blisters that leaked liquid iron oxide, and no matter how carefully you painted it, it would only look new for a month or two. Climb the circular stairs inside to the top walkway and you become an apostrophe atop a column of white and red concentric rings, some 350 feet above the water.

Up near the lens, the horizon is an absolutely straight and unforgiving line, except for the occasional uninterested passing ship. The joke about Cape Pine is that there are no pine trees anywhere near the light, anywhere on the cape—

no trees at all, unless you count scrubby alders and bog spruce. But it was a job, and when I took it, jobs were hard to find.

After I finished the dishes, and after I made the bed and took some meat out of the freezer for supper, I decided Madeline and the boys—Keiran's six now, and David's eight—might be down in Arnold Cove.

On a warm summer day in the afternoon when there's not much wind, it's almost idyllic down there. There's a stream that cuts down through the beach, and when the weather got really hot—years ago now, before I was keeper, when we used to drive down to the lighthouse and just dream—Madeline and I used to go swimming naked in the big freshwater pool under the overhanging cliff. I was always startled when she stood up, not by her nakedness or her breasts or her hips, but by the sharply defined V of her public hair. She could stand there as bold as brass, hands at her sides, and I'd have trouble tucking away the thought that I should really be looking away politely, officially pretending she had lost her suit in the current and somehow hadn't realized it yet. That she could stand there so simply, so boldly—it was like she'd been deposited here from another, faraway place, unaware of anything like convention.

Madeline's features are small and precise—like a porcelain teacup—but she has a way of looking at you that moves back and forth between innocent and downright feral. Her upper lip comes to a small double peak in the middle that she used to accentuate with bright red lipstick, and those two small points give her a look as if she is always up to something, a sort of impish, eager look, waiting for trouble. Mischievous.

In the heat, I could imagine her and the boys down bare-foot in the landwash, the waves rushing in fast along the grey sand and quickly ironing everyone's footprints away. Maybe building bonfires, although I couldn't smell any smoke. The wind wasn't exactly the right direction to bring the smoke back to the light, but I could see the cove, and there wasn't an obvious smudge rising up.

The walk to the cove is an easy one: half the ground is barrens, swept back and held in check by the constant wind. The highest vegetation is the August-yellowing strands of the cotton grass, and the wandering sheep pretty much take care of that. Paths wind into themselves, the tread of the sheep driven more by a search for food than by any partic-ular destination. But no tracks from little boys in the soft, peaty dips of the cove trail, no sign of the long, even lope of bare feet left by Madeline, even if I could easily imagine her walking along the path in the sun, her sneakers held by the laces in one swinging hand.

I knew that didn't mean they weren't at the cove. Made-line might have them all playing "Indian," making their way across the barrens without ever setting foot on a path, care-fully erasing anything like a human mark behind them. They might even be hiding along the spine of the next hummock, sighting at me with their hands over their eyes, seriously silent while I stumbled ignorantly towards them. They'd wait to the last moment and jump out at me, shouting "Surprise!"—all three of them, and they expect me to act surprised—which I always did, until they got so good at hiding that they would actually startle me, over and over again. The game stopped being even close to fun a long time ago. After a while, it just made me mad—in fact, angrier each and every time. I'd know they were out there watching me scrabble around, looking, and they'd all be up somewhere laughing to themselves.

Anyone could get mad about that, right?

Once, I came across all three of them walking backwards along the dust of the road, brushing away their tracks with scraps of spruce bough. They had walked straight down the middle of the road, avoiding the tire tracks so that it looked like our car had been the last thing to pass, walking lightly on the available patches of gravel and carefully obliterating any sign of their passing in the powdery dust.

Madeline had looked up impishly, a co-conspirator, dirt smeared on both sides of her narrow face. "You were lucky this time," she said. "We were almost out of sight."

Frustrated, I picked up a small rock and flung it hard at the ground. It took a strange carom, perhaps hitting another rock buried there in the dust, and it spun up off the ground and into her leg, opening a small cut above the point of her ankle that bled surprisingly freely. Looking up quickly at her eyes, I saw the flicker of pain, and then watched her eyes go pebble hard and shiny, like some sort of hidden shark's eyelid had come down.

"Like I said," Madeline whispered. "Lucky this time."

I'd had enough of the game. I turned and walked back to the tower.

Another time, I watched their bright shirts, two green, one red, from up on the catwalk around the tower where I was wiping the heavy salt spray off the glass, until, suddenly, when I looked over my shoulder, they were irretrievably gone. It was the kind of thing that makes you feel almost completely alone, makes you reach for the fridge and beer, even if it is barely afternoon on a Wednesday.

Arnold Cove is caught between cliffs, grey crumbling stone on one side, browning sheets of shale on the other. When the swell is just right, the waves roar directly in from the open ocean, shoulder high and cruel, the water collapsing and snatching itself back under. The small bay catches anything the ocean chooses to give up. There are plastic bottles up high at the tide line, discarded shoes, and the regular storm refuse of smashed lobster pots and buoys, along with the pieces of boats battered apart somewhere on distant and angry seas. Lost rubber red-orange Fireball work gloves, hopefully without hands inside, often lie palm up on the sand, begging attention.

As I made my way down the steep incline, there was no sign of Madeline and the boys. If they had somehow been transformed into white bleach bottles, I would have seen at least a dozen of them.

Once down on the beach, there was no real way to see if they were around. The tide was in, the water right up at the point where sand turns to fist-sized, jumbled round stones, and I couldn't see anywhere they'd left anything like a track. There were ash pits where old bonfires had been, but they were cold and smokeless, and when I dug my hands down into the ashes, they were rain wet, at least a few days old.

They probably weren't there. Bonfires were almost a given. Once down on the beach, Madeline likes to get the boys playing Cornish wrecker, and they need to get the bonfires big enough, they'd told me, "to lure the sailors to their watery deaths." Sometimes I can see huge clouds of smoke from the tower—big grey and black pillars of smoke. When I go down to see what they're doing, I can hear their whoops and shouts while I'm still far away on the path. They always stop as soon as they see me, and stand seriously warming their hands as the salt-dried sticks spit and flare and burn impossibly bright and hot. The wood is stripped by the salt and burns like rage; it's all fury and sheer flying-apart. Throw water onto one of their big beach fires and even the rocks underneath hiss and crack and explode in protest.

More than once, when I've started across the beach towards the fire, I've seen David move away and start skipping flat rocks out into the maws of the breaking waves, as intent on the surf as if counting the number of skips had become his full-time career. Keiran moves away then too, but not as far, leaving Madeline alone at the edge of the blaze, responsible for the pyre, her chin stuck out as if daring me to do something, her hair smelling of smoke.

I don't find it surprising that they have more in common with each other than they have with me. The cliffs are high and dangerous, and because of that, Madeline has spent virtually every waking minute with them, certainly every minute when they step outside the fence—supposed to keep the foraging sheep away from the tower and the house and the weather sampling station—and into the dangerous ground beyond.

The weather station is what takes most of my time. Other keepers didn't have to do as much with it, but several times a day I have to measure wind speeds and fog density and the thickness of freezing rain on the guy wires for the big signal tower. I have to log temperature and wind direction, even before making sure everything is running right, servicing the big triple foghorn and keeping the equipment in the tower in proper condition.

Once, I came down from working on the light's gears, cleaning out the old black fouled grease from between each tooth and packing in new lube with the grease gun, and found all three of them in the garden, Keiran little more than a toddler, David maybe five, collecting cabbage worms in empty paper drinking cups. Madeline was talking, telling the boys she was amazed how the cabbage white moths could find their way so far across the barrens to eat our cabbages, and I was struck for a moment by how much the fluttering, seemingly directionless flight of the moths reminded me of her.

Later, heading out to set the caterpillars free on the barrens, they left the gate open and the sheep got in and ate all the small plants right down to the ground, leaving only insolent black buttons of manure behind. I was furious when I found the gate swinging open and the plants—cabbage and carrots and potatoes—all gone, but Madeline just laughed and laughed and said, "Cabbage worms come in all sizes and some of them are woolly," and then started laughing at me, because I couldn't stop being angry, even when she put her hand up and ruffled my hair and said, "Woolly sheep, woolly sheep."

I pushed her then, a hand in each of the dips inside her shoulders, knocking her backwards into the fence and then down hard, flat on her back.

Afterwards, I said I was sorry.

I searched up and down the tide line, but they weren't there. I even went back up the brook behind the barrisway to the spot where they had had a lean-to earlier in the summer. The lean-to had fallen over, but there was still an apple juice can standing next to the firepit, its top cut off and a strand of heavy wire stretched across it to make a primitive tea kettle for boiled tea, all the paint burned off the outside and the rust furred and feasting on the burnt metal.

Madeline had spent one summer night alone out there with the boys after I said there was no point to camping when we were practically camping our whole lives anyway. But she had taken them out, all three loaded up with blankets, food and the good frying pan, and I watched them disappear down over the crest of the hill, then spent the rest of that evening drinking beer and throwing the empty bottles off the cliff to watch them tumble in the air and smash on the sharp rocks we were always telling the boys to avoid. When the wind and the angle of the bottle were just right, I'd get one thrumming whistle from the open neck as the bottle fell, coming back up through the air like a voice yelling an elongated and ever-fading "OOOooooo." Like the quiet version of the surprised sound you might hear if you came up behind someone and just pushed her quickly over the edge.

The third year we were at the Cape, Madeline knocked on our front door as if she were a stranger—as if there were ever any strangers out here—and I opened it to find her standing on the porch. She was wearing a short yellow summer dress, the wind picking at the hem, her feet and legs bare and scratched by the brush, holding a handful of fans of ground juniper boughs. The smell of the sap burst sharp off the branches, and the black berries made me think of gin.

"Surprise. Buy a bouquet for the lady?" she said, smiling, the words coming out in a put-on British accent.

So I brought her in and sat her down and got the first aid kit, wiping up the cross-hatched bloody lines on her legs and wondering where she had left her shoes. Some of the cuts were deep and jagged, where the thorns from the wild roses had caught and dragged, juddering, across her skin, leaving spots where the blood had risen, beaded and dried black. She just looked at me while I knelt there, cleaning her up. When I looked up, she was staring at me with a distracted, distant, half-smiling look, as if once again I had failed to grasp the point.

In the end, I forgot to put the juniper in water and the needles fell off all at once, leaving the grey and scaly branches looking like the limbs of an animal that had died and then shed its fur.

The next morning, I woke up alone in bed. Madeline said she had been so tired that she'd fallen asleep on the couch. David told me later—quietly, in that small boy's singsong voice and with his eyes darting back and forth as if he was betraying a confidence—that she had spent the night in his bed, that they were crew on a sailing ship bound for port in France. The gale that came up outside that night had been ripping the sky like fabric, so I told him that any sailing ship near us would have been blasted far, far away by just one breath of savage wind, and would've sunk. All hands lost.

I hit her in the face—hard—on a hot July morning when she was three steps up from the bottom of the circular staircase in the light tower. I just pulled my arm back and waited, and then let it go as soon as she was in range.

Madeline sat down sharply on the metal step.

"Surprise," I said. I thought I'd made my voice sound light enough, as if I were joking.

I had been standing off on the edge of the stairs, and Madeline had come in out of the bright summer sunlight, blinking in the sudden change from light to gloom. If I'd really meant to hurt her, I would have waited until she was farther up the stairs, so that the fall would have been even worse than the punch.

I watched her nose begin to bleed in the shadows, a dark line running down from each nostril, waiting to hear just one more smart-mouthed word. Instead, I watched all the mischief seep away, right there in front of me. Watched it empty out until she didn't even look like herself. Then I turned and walked up the stairs.

I may have hit her before, maybe a few times, but it was only out of frustration, and it wasn't ever as hard as that, and she hadn't looked like that afterwards. It hadn't ever been quite like this. But it wasn't my fault.

They had been gone all day on a mission because Madeline had heard on the radio about new fossils found at Mistaken Point, and while they were gone I'd been doing everything. I'd done laundry and dishes in the house, finding my own lunch when they still hadn't come back halfway through the day. Wrestling with the wrong-sized wrenches in the tower, working on the gear train, barking my knuckles when the wrenches slipped, unable to get into town and find the right-sized sockets because I didn't have the car. I had the right wrenches somewhere, but I couldn't find them: Madeline and the boys had gotten tired of hiding themselves, and their new game was hiding things like tools. I'd see something shiny sticking out of the rock wall below the tower and find a pair of Vise-Grips stashed in there almost out of sight. I told them that it wasn't funny, that it was dangerous if anything happened and I couldn't set the light, that there were ships and sailors depending on us, but they laughed, Keiran doubled over, laughing so hard that it looked like he might pee in his pants.

"If they wreck on our beach," David said seriously, "we'll go on board and steal their shoes and their clock and their bare-o-meter."

I told him he had no idea what a barometer even was.

They'd gone on their fossil exploration and I was working away, getting more and more angry, waiting for them to come back, knowing I'd probably have my head under something when they all charged in and startled me again. The more I thought about it, the better idea it seemed to be to have a surprise of my own. That's why I met Madeline in the dark, coming up the stairs, probably hoping to startle me again. It was not the best idea to hit her, but really, it's not all my fault.

When I came up out of Arnold Cove on a long, careful loop, still looking for them, I was miles out of the way and soaked to my knees from crossing the caribou bog. It was hot enough that I at least knew I wasn't likely to get caught in a sudden fog. I could see the tip of the light tower, but that was almost the only familiar landmark.

The barrens are low, rolling hummocks of peat, each hummock hiding more hummocks out behind. It's easy to lose your way, but at least I had the tower far off to my right, and I was pretty sure, wherever they were hiding this time, I had to be far enough out to be clearly behind them. I knew they wouldn't expect that: their little game depended on their knowing the direction I'd be coming from, and I wanted them with their backs to me, stretched out flat on one of the drier, higher mounds, oblivious to the fact that I was close until I was right on top of them.

I had fallen hard climbing up out of the valley, and that was on grey slippery rocks, gashing my shin through my already wet trousers. I went into a boghole, deep treacle-wet peat, and I remember wondering how it was that the caribou that make the barrens home don't break their legs getting around. You see them in the distance regularly, the caribou, ragged white and light brown cotton tufts gathered together in groups of twenty or so, like scarecrows with their clothes coming apart and their stuffing coming out. Usually there are ten or so down on their chests; the others are up and feeding, but there's always one or two that are alert and looking around, making sure that nothing is sneaking up on them. It's like they set up their own broad perimeter, watching out in all directions for any unexpected movement. They don't care if you can see them, as long as they've already seen you first. And then they always move off as soon as you try to get too close.

I wrenched my knee badly in the third fall. By then I was too angry and tired to be careful.

The ground on the barrens is uneven; the walking jars your knees and ankles as you stagger from dip to moss mount, and I was already streaming with sweat. Around my face and above my head, the biting stouts had caught my scent, and the big deer flies were endlessly circling my head, waiting for the right chance to draw blood.

I put a foot wrong as I was going over a pile of loose rocks, then put the other foot down through a screen of juniper covering a deep hole. I teetered over and fell sideways, feeling my knee give out. As I fell and before the pain started, I felt a curious ripping in my knee, like the feeling of tearing heavy corrugated cardboard crosswise. When I stood up, there was a sharp pain the moment I put weight on my leg, and I sat down again, almost crying out. I sat for a while, ripping up bog plants with my fists, tearing apart any flower stalk I could reach.

It was her goddamned fault, I thought. This was her fucking game and her fucking fault. I was out sitting on my butt on the barrens and they'd all think it was a big fucking joke. I remember thinking there'd have to be payback for this.

It's time they realized just how goddamn serious it really was.

As soon as I got moving again, I went straight through the bog covering a small pond. Falling forwards, my leg still stuck out straight, I knew I was going into the water the moment the bog gave way.

Suddenly swimming, I had a moment of sheer panic when it seemed like I wouldn't be able to get back out. I was flailing around, tearing apart the bog, trying to find solid ground. When I tried to stand, I sank into the gluey, peaty black silt at the bottom, and I couldn't seem to reach the edge. My injured leg was screaming as I tried to stay afloat, and I thought that this time they'd actually killed me with their stupid game.

Madeline should have known better. I had wasted the whole day looking for them, and that meant the weather observations hadn't been done—no temperatures, no wind speeds. Now I'd get a careful message from St. John's or Gander, questioning whether the system was down or whether their keeper was passed out drunk in his own kitchen again.

Eventually I got out of the bog, but I was soaking wet, my clothes shot through with peat, and I had dragged myself across the bog with my hands until I could finally stand. Even then, heading straight for the tower with my knee swollen and throbbing, it took me almost two hours to get back.

I didn't even care if they were watching me anymore, didn't care if they caught me or tried to startle me. They just better not come within reach. If I got back to the house and they were already comfortably back, I'd put the place up, I swore I would.

But the house was quiet.

By then, it was cooling a little outside, a light wind had come up, and I could see the front edge of fog rolling in. If I'd been caught out in that, I thought, I'd be on the barrens until the weather finally broke. And that could be days, if the wind was right.

They weren't upstairs, and I was pretty sure they weren't in the basement either, although I wasn't going to hazard the stairs to find out, not with a knee that had swollen to the size of a grapefruit. It took me ages to get my wet jeans down over the swelling, and I threw all of the filthy, soaking clothes down the stairs to the concrete basement.

Let her deal with it, I thought. It's her fault anyway.

I had a beer and then another, throwing the caps at the sink, sitting at the kitchen table and looking around, trying to decide when they'd be back, or if they'd been back already. It would be just like Madeline to take the boys into Trepassey for fish and chips and leave me on my own for a cold dinner of whatever I could scrape up from leftovers in the fridge.

After a while, I staggered around the house, trying to find any sign of where they might be. I ended up in our bedroom in front of the dresser.

I opened her top drawer, to see if the laundry had been done yet, to see if she had found the laundry basket down by the washer and had brought it back up, socks and underwear nestled down into their proper spaces.

The drawer was empty. Completely empty, as it had been since the day they'd gone to Mistaken Point and we'd met on the stairs. Just like every other drawer on her side of the dresser. Only the paper on the bottom, and the dry green smell of birch. I hit the dresser with my fist, over and over, because there was nothing else left to do.

I went to the boys' rooms, where the pillows never moved and the covers were never thrown back, the beds always made and never slept in. Where stuffed animals had decamped for other pastures.

And I remembered a month earlier watching from the tower and seeing the back of Madeline's head as she drove away—the boys too small for their heads to even show up in the back window of the car—the dust from the tires kicking up into the air in a grey-brown rooster tail and blowing away to the right of the road, disappearing in among the leaves of the blueberry bushes and rhodora.

Surprise.

SHARP CORNER

*J*OHN thought of the sound as a soft, in-drawn breath, a breath that was always taken in that last single second before the other sounds came. He heard it right before the shriek of tires pulling sideways against their tread. John would hear the police use the word "yaw" for the striated mark left behind on the pavement, and he'd start building it into his own descriptions almost immediately. "When you see yaw, you know they were going too fast." Just like that.

The tires made a shriek followed by the boxy thump of the car fetching up solid, side-on, in a crumpling great pile in the ditch.

Then, the horn—and often, screaming.

The mailbox at the end of the driveway had his last name, Eckers, in precisely placed stick-on block letters. It was John and Mary's second mailbox this year. Along the front of the property he could still see the places where he had planted a regimented row of seven maples. Only one of the original trees remained, its leaves in late autumn blaze, and it was the tree down at the very edge of the property. The rest had been sheared off by a red Suzuki Sidekick, three teenagers and the unforgiving shallow turn in the road just at the end of the driveway.

"Three times?" other people would ask at parties, disbelief making their voices rise high at the ends of their sentences. "Cars have crashed three times right in front of your house?"

"Third time unlucky," John would say wryly, as if the sentence had just occurred to him, as if it was a bitter turn of phrase that had sprung just then from quick personal reflection, and then he'd start talking about the sounds, the smells.

He had spent two days planting the trees—staking out the straight line, digging the holes, preparing the wet clay with buckets of topsoil so the trees would have at least a chance to get started and eventually grow into a stately line. He imagined the trees as much more than saplings, imagined Mary looking out the big front windows on the front of their bungalow, watching for the bright yellow of the school bus through the tightly woven leaves, waiting for it to pull to a stop. Every time, he imagined she had a dishcloth in her hands, imagined she was working the damp fabric around something as she stared out through the glass. The house was well back from the road, a small three-bedroom ranch, just one of dozens like it along the narrow highway.

No kids yet, but they were hoping. It was a hope that he almost had trouble figuring out. It was, he thought, as if he and Mary needed some particular completion that they just couldn't find otherwise; that they felt there was something missing, something they kept looking for, and that they had loosely decided must rest in starting a family.

In an offhand way, he thought it was like the trees. Other people had trees, big, tall, dignified trees like footnotes to their complete and satisfied lives. It's what you get when you're diligent and careful and you plan ahead. Like children—and then grandchildren. Get kids, and then you get grandchildren too. He'd tried to explain that to Mary as if it was all a given, but she didn't seem to get it at all.

Sometimes, he imagined himself as an old man, raking up the fallen leaves around maple trunks as thick as a man's waist. He had planted the trees far enough apart to take that into consideration, and he had researched how much space a mature maple needs, reading up on different tree species before making his final choice. He imagined kids running around too, kids who could safely be packed up at the end of the day and sent home.

The Suzuki ended any chance of that. Late on a Friday night, the car spent its last few seconds in the air, completing a shallow but complex barrel roll to the right. John found out later it was three clean, tight and acrobatic rotations, while inside the metal box everything flew around along its own personal imperative, physics moving scores of things in hundreds of directions. A dozen beer on the back seat didn't manage to escape the cardboard confines of their box, but every single bottle broke its neck hitting the roof of the car, a roof that was now sharply lower after the touchdown on the first spin. A carton of paperback books in the back, taped and Magic Markered and designated for a church sale, burst their bounds and the books battered around inside the back of the car, fluttering wildly. All the floor mats leapt up an inch or two and then settled topographically back into ridges and valleys, the dips catching the diamonds of safety glass from the broken side windows.

John would find the spare tire the next morning, almost up to the side of the house, long after the wrecker had dragged away all the other pieces.

One of the teens left the car too, winding up spread-eagled on the lawn, but it was the firefighters who found him. John didn't even realize the teen was there until they'd put the boy on a gurney and brought him down the driveway.

The crash was, John decided, the most gruesome thing he had ever seen. He and Mary had been in the living room, watching television, when the Suzuki first left the road. For just an instant, Mary had reached across and set her hand on his wrist, but John was up off the couch in a moment, looking out at the black silhouette in the yard, backlit by the street lights, the car's headlights still pooling on the grass.

When he was out the door and standing next to the wreck, his pulse hammered quickly in a not unpleasant way, and he could feel it tripping hard in his ears.

Mary stayed in the house.

John had approached the car gingerly, as if there were some need to treat the overturned vehicle gently. He could hear the exhaust system ticking as the metal cooled, the pace of the ticks slowing.

One of the teenagers left inside the car had been thrown upwards in virtually the same arc as the beer case. The stem of the rear-view mirror had taken out his left eye, but it didn't matter. His neck was broken along the same angle as all the bottles.

The driver, meanwhile, met the steering wheel with his chest, the roof with his shoulder and the inside of the door with the ribs of his left side—except for his left arm, which flicked out through the broken window as if signalling a turn and then snapped as the car rolled smoothly over it. A Kleenex box and a dozen CDs had flown through the air, striking things and flying again. With the last thump, the glove compartment had burst open, vomiting paper and a windshield scraper and a spare house key that everyone in the owner's family had been trying to find for months.

The first thing John noticed as he came down the driveway was how cleanly the tumbling vehicle had sheared off six of his seven maples. The mailbox post was snapped off at ground level. The mailbox itself, crushed, turned up underneath the car once it was finally moved.

In the minutes before the emergency crews arrived— Mary had called 911, standing in the front window like a black cut-out of herself—John decided both of the teenagers in the car had to be dead. He was wrong. The driver survived, as did the passenger from the back seat, the passenger who had popped out through the back window after the glass burst away and who had flown, wingless, to crumple in the grass.

John stood rooted in one spot when the fire trucks arrived, stunned by the lights and the noise and the rapid, clipped motion of the firefighters. He was still standing in the same place when the police, finished with their brief investigation, their measurements and photographs, stopped traffic in both directions so the wrecker, parked square across the road, could stand the vehicle back on its wheels, drag it back onto the road and haul the wreck away.

It seemed like it was over in minutes, but Mary told him he had been outdoors for more than an hour and a half. That was all she said. After that, she didn't want to talk about it anymore.

John couldn't understand why. He tried to talk to Mary about it, about the long gouge in the grass and the way the mailbox was carried along by the car and then pancaked flat, about the teenagers and the way they'd looked and the fact he hadn't even realized one of them was launched clear and had been lying on the grass of the front yard like he was having a nap.

Mary listened for a few minutes, but as soon as she heard that one of the teenagers had died, she abruptly told him that she had no interest in hearing any more about it.

He found that somehow discouraging.

Mary was a small woman, and the two of them made an incongruous pair. Some couples look like each other, but John and Mary didn't. He was tall and thin, with dark, straight hair, his face too sharp for his own liking. Once, upon inspection in the mirror, he had decided his eyes were too close together. Mary, on the other hand, was small and doll-like and perfectly balanced, with big eyes that always seemed to be perched on the verge of surprise. The difference between them actually made him uncomfortable. People, he thought, might look at them and find it hard to believe they belonged together, especially when they heard Mary talk, heard the way her words came out tiny and precise and high, like a child's.

Although John never told her, he found hearing her thin, small voice when they made love both thrilling and somehow illicit, the same kind of forbidden pleasure, he imagined, as the idea of seducing a teen babysitter.

Maybe people just get used to looking at their families, he thought, and end up predisposed to liking someone else whose face falls into familiar lines and expressions. It wasn't that way with Mary, so sometimes he found himself holding her hand desperately, or throwing an arm across her shoulders at a party, just to prove how made for each other they really were. Sometimes he just held her arm, his hand tight, oblivious to the fact that she wanted to shake free and couldn't.

He took her out to dinner the night after the accident. And then he found himself talking about it all evening, words spilling out of him all at once. John felt the occasional stab of guilt for keeping her pinned in the chair, unable to just get up and leave because they were in public. But he kept talking anyway, and part of him enjoyed the way he could make her flinch with the more graphic details. Later that night he reached for her in bed, but she rolled away from him, curling in on herself, and before he fell asleep, he thought for a short, distracted moment that she might be crying.

With the second crash—dry, clear roads, right in the middle of a sunny Sunday afternoon—John felt he'd gotten better at grasping the important details. At cataloguing them more carefully. This time it was a pickup truck with a load of freshly cut fir logs. It didn't so much leave the road as trundle in a straight line off hard into the ditch, the truck stopping faster than its load of wood did.

The top layer of logs slid through the window behind the driver, with one log, slightly more than a foot in diameter, striking the driver right at the base of the skull before smashing out through the windshield and coming to a stop on the hood. John stared through the side window at the driver for ages, amazed at the fact that the man's dead hands were still holding on to the wheel, waiting fruitlessly for a signal to let go.

The passenger, a man in his fifties, was turned in his seat, caught as if looking at the driver, staring across "stone dead," John would say later, as if killed by the tableau of sheer horror sitting next to him.

When the ambulance crew arrived a handful of minutes later, they yanked the passenger out of the truck roughly and spread him flat on his back on the ground, surrounded by John's freshly cut grass, futilely pushing on the man's chest and pumping air into his lungs with a ribbed plastic bag. John watched across the hood of the truck, smelling both the crisp smell of the fir sap and the brassy sharp tang of the fresh blood. He watched as the fire crew unloaded their gear, cut the roof away with the tools and lifted the log off the mangled driver.

This time, he had a better idea about everything the firefighters were doing, and when the police arrived, he realized that their investigation was more involved than he had given them credit for the first time. The whole process was quick, sure, but more calculated than he had realized with the Suzuki. They measured the short skid that lipped over the white line at the edge of the road and down into the gravel shoulder, and one policeman took photographs from every conceivable angle, stopping the firefighters at one point so that he could record the pattern left in the glass where the logs had marked and sprung through the back window. They unrolled a long yellow measuring tape and measured from the back wheels of the truck to where the skid started, and one officer climbed the tailgate and photographed the logs, too.

It wasn't just the investigation that was more involved. John thought all the colours were brighter too, and the sounds more distinct—the reds and greens, the leaves and the oozing bark, and the way everyone moved quietly, voices low, as if the seriousness demanded silence. There was the way the sun caught at the scattered glass that had burst out onto the hood, the way the spiderweb of cracks in the glass worked their way ever wider apart as they moved from the point where the log had come out through the windshield. John recognized the sharp smell of the diesel exhaust of the fire trucks, and the sound of the grumble of the big engine in the ambulance, idling. He could smell gasoline from somewhere under the truck, and the heavy, more involved scent of motor oil too, and he was still staring when the driver's son arrived in his own car, leaping out and running to the pickup until the firefighters got in his way and pushed him back to where the police were taking notes.

John watched as the man sat in the back of the police cruiser, thunking his head rhythmically against the Plexiglas divider between the front and back seats. And all at once John thought he had to start gathering every piece he could, as if there were a great importance hidden in every scrap of it. He was keenly aware how hard it was to catch all the small things; there was just so much going on. There was a green deodorant tree hanging on a thin string from the rear-view mirror of the truck. You couldn't make that kind of irony up, he thought, the driver obviously trying to import the smell of evergreens right into the cab. And then he'd managed to do exactly that.

The paramedics had cut the shirt away from the passenger's stomach and chest, and his arms and legs were stretched out like he was trying to catch something huge falling out of the sky—and the front of the man's pants were soaking wet.

Maybe, John thought, it would help if I took my own photographs.

Whenever they went out socially, the topic of the accidents always seemed to come up. What was it like to have people regularly dying at the end of your driveway?

John surprised even himself: he started talking about the crashes almost every time he and Mary went out, and he was always amazed by the way strangers would circle tight around him as the stories got more detailed. It brought a sudden importance to the room, an obvious and almost respectful hush. John learned as he went along that it was better if he didn't tell the whole story in one go, but instead kept things back, parcelling details out piece by piece, always making the careful effort to keep his face earnest, sincere, almost shaken. Better still if he could make it seem as if he didn't really want to have to talk about it—as if others were dragging the gruesome details out of him against his will. Almost as if he were suggesting throughout that it was their own fault—"You wanted to hear this"—while at the same time the stories were beginning to fall into a carefully practised pattern, a kind of rote. Trying to remember if he was talking to people who'd heard the stories before.

Working on the highs and the lows, the beginnings, midpoints and ends—the careful pacing.

The punchlines.

John learned when to pause seriously and look down, letting the words fall out of his mouth like they were too heavy to hold in—"they were both dead"—and when he should stare intently at one of the listeners and make his eyes as large as he could, as if astounded by the sheer wonders of car-crash physics and geometry.

"Not a mark on him," he'd say about the passenger in the pickup. "Not a mark."

Then he'd wait, wait and force his audience to make him tell them about the horror of the driver, about what it looked like when the top logs in the pile barrelled into the back of his head and shoulders through the flat glass of the pickup's back window.

It was, he thought, a lot like fishing: you could feel the listeners coming closer and closer to the hook, nipping, swirling, and all the time he'd be waiting for his opportunity to strike it home and watch them flinch, watch their eyes dart away because they couldn't take it after all.

He'd be discouraged, sometimes, when the listeners suddenly lost interest and turned away, or if they didn't ask the right question so that he could say something to well and truly crush their curiosity. But he learned more every time, with every telling of the story.

Once, at an anniversary party for a couple they'd never see socially again, he had been in full flight, describing the familiar flattened mailbox and the way it had been mowed over twice—and then the teenager who had lost both his eye and his life—when he glimpsed Mary, just close enough to hear him at the edge of the circle of listeners, her face mapped hard with disgust. The hosts had already fled into the kitchen, the door swinging shut behind them, looking for more hors d'oeuvres that no one was going to want to eat.

That night, in their bedroom, she was furious with him. He couldn't see her, all the lights out and the curtains pulled tight, but her words in the darkness were so sharp that he imagined they had to come from someone else.

"I hate it," Mary hissed at him, and John could imagine the words hanging in the air, white block capitals against the dark, disconnected from anything else. "Every time, everywhere we go, it's the same damn stories. And you always look so smug, like you're cashing in on someone else's misfortune. I wish you could see yourself. You've turned into a vulture." Then, in smaller letters that hung in the air for even longer: "Sometimes I don't even like you anymore, John."

He imagined the words fading away in the air, their edges dissolving.

But he didn't answer, caught up in just part of what she had said.

Smug, he thought. Now that stung.

So when he was shaving, he practised making the right kind of face. It had to be a combination of serious and resigned, he thought, moving his eyebrows up and down but failing to find just the pattern he was looking for. He was reaching for dignified, with a touch of something like respect for the fallen thrown in. As far away from smug as he could make it.

The third crash was different—not quite in their yard this time, but caused by too much speed on the same familiar straightaway, and by the same sharp curve just before the house. A car had swung its way almost into the ditch, one front wheel over onto the loose stones of the shoulder, but this time the driver had cut the wheel sharply, in time to get his car back onto the road. He was successful in that, but in the process he flung his car across the centre line and straight into the path of a dump truck heading in the opposite direction. Neither driver had a chance to react after that, and the accident was awesome in its sheer brutality.

There were no pieces travelling around the car in their delicate prescribed arcs, finding their way to a new position along explainable lines. This was all hard, full, spectacular stop, the car crumpling abruptly underneath the huge engine of the truck, the back of the car accordioning into the front as it kept moving forwards.

Inside the house, the head-on impact sounded like an explosion. John jumped off the couch, knowing immediately what had happened. As he ran for the door, Mary threw the book she had been reading at him, the pages whiffling and fluttering, but she missed.

John could see how serious the accident was as soon as he got out the door. It was the way the dump truck was crouched over the crushed car like a cat over a small and absolutely dead mouse. The driver's door on the truck was open, the driver running around the car from one side to the other, trying to see inside. The roof, what you could see of it, was crushed flat down to the tops of the doors, so the vehicle looked more like a sheet-steel tank than anything else.

There was an absolute absence of sound, everything startled into silence.

John could see that other cars were stopping, people piling out in a rush until they got close enough to the car to take a good look. Then they were simply slumping away, leaning on their cars as if they needed the support, as if their bones and muscles had suddenly developed an inexplicable weakness.

Glass was thrown out and away from the car in all directions, every single mirror and window broken explosively so that the pieces were intermingled in a great wide circle all around the car.

Then the dump truck driver was sitting on the ground in shock, his face covered with his hands and his back against the front wheel of the truck. He was moaning, his legs thrown out in front of him as if he'd lost the ability to move at all. Something was oozing from the bottom of the crushed car, but John was too far away to tell whether it was blood or transmission fluid. Later, he'd decide it had to be blood. It sounded better that way.

Up close, it was hard to make out anything, and it wasn't until he heard the details on the news that it was clear there had been three people in the car—and that all of them were dead. The car was so totally destroyed that John had a hard time deciding just what it was he was looking at—but that confusion would shrink with each telling of the story, the details settling themselves more solidly every time through.

Minutes after the fire trucks roared down the road and stopped, John saw a firefighter step away from the side of the car, walk across the road, bend at the waist and carefully throw up in the ditch.

John found himself edging in far closer than he ever had before, and he felt almost offended when one of the firefighters rudely pushed him back out of the way. "If you'd just step back a bit, sir," the firefighter said, but John found the "sir" hard and sharp, as if the firefighter was also making some kind of judgment he didn't appreciate.

There was occasional steam coming from the front of the car, and the two front wheels had disappeared under the dump truck. There were long, slow discussions among the firefighters about the best way to move the heavy truck. They had managed to lift enough of the roof on one side of the car to peer carefully inside the flattened wreck. No one was rushing anymore.

John was still caught up in the sheer drama of the scene when a newspaper reporter saw him and came over, asking questions about the crash. It was strange how much John enjoyed that, he thought later. But he *had* enjoyed it, enjoyed it tremendously, all the while keeping his face as respectful as he could, telling the reporter about the seriousness of the crash, about all three of the crashes, leading the reporter up across the lawn to show him the healing scar in the grass and the sharp stumps, now starting to turn grey, of the clipped-off maples, agreeing when the reporter asked if his photographer could take John's picture for the story he was doing.

The next day, they had put his picture with the story on the bottom of the front page, and John thought he looked properly solemn and not the least bit smug at all. Turning to the obituaries and holding the paper up in front of him, John wondered if he should go to the funerals. He imagined standing there in church, formally dressed, impassive yet serious, while family members nudged each other and looked over at the man they'd seen in the paper. The unfortunate guy with three fatal crashes right in his yard. The guy who had tried to help. Somehow, John had managed to convince himself that standing there was included in helping. In the end, he thought better of going to the funerals. It would take far too much time out of the day, he thought.

The latest crash was, without a doubt, the best story yet. John could tell the first time he told it. He could tell by the way his listeners' faces fell, everyone standing in a small circle holding their drinks while the last barbecue of the year heated and smoked behind them, steaks forgotten. It was late in the year, the evenings already sharp and suddenly cold, the sky grey with impending sleet. There was always someone, John thought, who just couldn't let go, who had to keep the summer going. So there were steaks and burgers, sweaters and jackets pulled around tight, and blue smoke blowing sideways away from the barbecue while John held a beer and talked gravely about the latest accident.

"So he cut the wheel back—and that was the right thing to do, cut the wheel back, and get out of the skid—but he went too far with it, and there was this dump truck," John said, listening to himself as he talked.

Tone it down, he told himself, pull back—not so preachy.

"Not survivable," saying it like a judge delivering a verdict. "I could tell that right away. You didn't even have to run—nothing anyone could have done anyway.

"Crushed them right there where they were sitting, even the kid in the back seat. Hard to even tell what parts belonged to which body."

John hadn't even seen the bodies—the police had come and taped off the scene after the firefighter had pushed him back, closing the road and holding up tarpaulins when the firefighters started cutting the car into pieces—but nobody knew that.

John thought about throwing in a resigned shrug, then thought better of it. He caught a glimpse of Mary's eyes, and they looked sharp and beady and black like a crow's.

Afterwards, when they'd left for home in the car, she started talking, her voice low, her face fixed and straight ahead so that she was talking to him without ever looking at him. "You enjoy it too much," she said. "All these horrible things that happened to other people." Her hands were working in her lap as if desperately trying to find something to do, he thought, or as if she was afraid he might hit her.

"Don't be foolish," he said sharply. "I don't enjoy anything about it."

She didn't answer.

"Really, how could I enjoy it? Do you think I like it, having to go down there again and again? The kind of things I've seen, Mary—you have no idea." John could feel the roundness of the words filling him up and spilling out, their order rhythmic and patterned and familiar, knowing when to carefully let his voice fall and crumble a bit at the end of the sentence.

She hadn't come out of the house, he thought, not even once, so she had no right to lecture him at all.

Mary watched his face out of the corner of her eye, recognizing the practised ease of his expressions flowing from one into another, an actor reprising his role.

"How could I like it?" John went on. "Do you think I like dragging some dead guy out of his truck to do CPR on him on the lawn? Having to go out in my own yard and find some teenager out there like a rag-doll roadkill or something? How could I like that, Mary?"

He loved that last little bit of alliteration—*rag-doll roadkill*—liked it so much that he'd used it every single time since the first time the tough-sounding words had accidentally tumbled out when he'd been searching for the right description.

He was only pausing for effect, for breath, but she cut him off. "You've never done CPR on anyone," Mary said quietly. "And you don't have to do this with me." She paused, but before he could say anything else, her thin, small voice said, "John—I don't think I can do this anymore."

The words were fine and distinct and set down formally in place like dishes on a dining room table, forks and knives in order, napkins square. Planned.

John stopped talking then and held the steering wheel tightly with both hands, telling himself that if anyone knew how important it was to stay focused when you were driving, it had to be him. After they'd driven a bit farther, he tried to reach across for her hand, but he couldn't find it in the dark of the front seat. When his fingers grazed her wrist, Mary snatched her arm away.

Home, and the freezing rain that had been threatening finally arrived. The sleet was travelling through the lights outside the house in ragged sheets, and the last scraps of fall were being torn down from the trees and thrown around the yard by the wind. Sitting in the living room in the dark, John could hear the change in the tone of the raindrops, could hear the glassy flexing of the iced power lines moving in the wind. No salt trucks yet—they always get out slowly on a Saturday night, he thought. Bound to be slippery out there, and the turn is always sharper than it seems.

He quietly moved the muscles in his arms and legs, flexing and relaxing them, imagining each group of muscles getting ready to run. Mary washing her face in the bathroom, turning off the light, closing the bedroom door with what John thought had to be an accusing click.

He heard the wet tires of every passing car, imagining that he heard them spin and grip, and spin and grip again. And every time, as every car came closer, he drew in one long and quiet breath and held it, the way a sigh might sound in reverse. Waiting. Ready for when he'd be called upon.

After every car passed, he'd breathe again.

OPEN ARMS

"*A*T THE SOUND of the beep, leave a message."
So I do.

It's in shorthand, I realize afterwards, because by now he should be more than able to read between all the lines. By now he should be able to read me too.

"I don't need any of my high school transcripts anymore, right? Or my grade six report card? I mean, there's no reason I would—who would want to see them? We took three truck-loads of stuff to the dump. The painting's going to be fine, but there's rain coming now." The hiss of the recorder. "It's Mary. Okay, you know that. Gimme a call."

After I hang up, I realize how disjointed the message must sound, how I've been talking while at the same time turning slowly around in my living room, my eyes and my words catching on things as I pass over them. I almost pick up the phone again and call back, but I stop myself. I want to call back and say, "I love you and I miss you, and you still want to be with me, right?" It's awful to sound so desperate, so eager, so needy, but I need the reassurance more than ever.

I need to hear him laugh, that almost dismissive two-step chuckle. It's a laugh that feels like your hair's being ruffled condescendingly, like someone wrapping their arms around a child or bending carefully down so they can talk face to face.

I need him to pick up the phone so I know he's really there. I'm sure he's caught the note in my voice that says I need him, even if there isn't anything obvious about it in the words I've said.

I can imagine the answering machine coming on in his new place, springing to robotic life. I can see that small apartment in the shorthand he's given me—the yellow paint and wooden floors and no pictures on the walls, so that the whole place sits in my mind like an image from a real estate website.

Oh yes, that's right: the apartment he hasn't said I should come over and see yet.

He's told me the people downstairs cook big dinners most weekends, whole turkeys sometimes, or roast beef with potatoes, so that the whole place smells like someone's mother's house. The other tenants all seem to have big, deep-bellied voices, though he's not sure whether it's really them or whether it's just the acoustics of their kitchen and hall. I can't picture the bathroom or the kitchen that's also his laundry room, even though his neighbours stumble constantly through my thoughts like big-footed trolls.

I imagine my own warbled words coming out through his answering machine and battering around the room like restless little birds, distressed and panicked and bouncing from room to room, looking only for his ears so they can settle.

Every now and then, I worry about him naked on a bed in a room I haven't yet seen, another woman in there, panting and eager and under him, and I force that image out of my head as quickly as I can, telling myself that my doubts are all about me and my damaged sense of trust, clearly much more about me than him. But this move, this step, is all much harder than I thought it would be.

I don't know what I thought. I don't know why I thought it. I guess I thought we would come together like some sort of relentless force, that our lives would just melt together— not easily, not seamlessly, but as if they were always intended to and were just now getting around to it.

When I call again, he's still not home, and I try to keep my voice level. "I didn't expect it to be like this, okay? I mean, I'm out here taking my whole life through the door in cardboard boxes. I guess I thought I'd be past worrying, that it wouldn't just seem so final. But I'm out of my depth here."

I listen to the phone after I finish, but I hear only the empty line and then the click when the machine hangs up. I pretend that it's exactly the same click in his living room as it is in mine, that the end of the call is as unifying as it is dividing.

I've never liked this house. Never. It was a stopgap for me and for the girls, a stepping stone, a way station that was supposed to be on the way to him.

I bought it for a reasonable enough price. Small, in a nice enough neighbourhood, but nothing magic. Nothing magic at all. Under other circumstances, if I had been planning to stay in it for longer, I wouldn't have even considered buying it. It wouldn't have even been on my list as a possibility. It would have been discarded after a look from the pavement outside, or at best, after the door opened and I got the combination of smell and light—just the overall sense of the place. But I was running from the latest mistake. Retrenching again. Putting up walls, and setting my defences against the next relationship that could go wrong. So I grabbed the first safe place I could get my hands on, the first one that was in reach.

It's a capable house. It's a house that is all the words you'd never want written in a performance evaluation at work, the kind of words no one expects to have applied to themselves. Workmanlike. Satisfactory. On time. On budget. This house has all of the pieces to do the job, and absolutely nothing more.

It's green clapboard, with a sharp, short peak to the roof, small rooms and low ceilings. It only has a postage stamp of a yard, just enough for me to work my way around with a push mower in ten minutes and be finished.

I can imagine what people would say if they were potential buyers, driving down the street and seeing it sitting there, another nondescript one of a row of suitable, no-frills homes. The same dismissive kinds of words his wife's friends would find to apply to me: "Blond, bottle blond probably, just what you might have expected. And cheap. Low rent."

I get it. Bad neighbourhood. Crooked teeth. Leaking shingles.

Whatever.

The way I like to think about it, her friends would be the people who only come to snoop around at the open house. They're never going to buy anyway—they're here to trash the place with words, to finger the fabric of the curtains and make fun of the people in the photos on the mantel and the knick-knacks on the side tables.

Michael and I once ate a big brunch in a diner near my house. It's the kind of place where there's still Formica on the table-tops, the edges finished with an aluminum band screwed into place, red Naugahyde benches you slide into sideways when you sit down. Good-tasting food that's bad for you. We wrote down our financial plans on paper napkins: how much we would be making, what kind of house we could afford, what kind of nest egg I could get out of the house when I sold it. How it would bring our joint mortgage payment down, because we'd have a house and mortgage together by then. Figuring out that it was all possible—how it was almost easy. On paper, anyway.

It all came down to graphite numbers on paper napkins, numbers that were all smudged when I pulled the napkin out of my purse weeks later and realized budgets couldn't change anything, as long as they were in my purse instead of his hands.

Outside the restaurant that morning, the snow was pil-ing in against the window like it was trying to force its way inside, its leading edge discovering the warm glass then crumpling all at once and sliding wetly down.

Scrambled eggs and ham fried flat, one lone sausage that came to the table on the plate with all the other food but still managed to look ostracized and lonely. Hash browns that were already cold, the whole meal resolute about not living up to its promise. The waitress who had taken our orders stood with her back towards us, forestalling any chance at complaint. She was flirting with the cook most of the time we were there, coming back to the table only to quickly slosh more coffee into our cups.

I wound up doing most of the talking that day and all of the writing down, the math all careful and accurate. I remember making a mistake and trying to erase it, the eraser biting down through the paper all the way to blood-red Formica, like opening a wound.

My house has got to sell, and it's got to sell for a high price. I need all of the down payment back, and more on top if I can get it.

I keep telling the girls that it has to sell high, forcing them into the bathroom to cut out and replace the caulking around the tub, to clean floor tiles for prospective buyers they've never even met, so it's like they were asked to get down on their knees and pray there to Mammon or the Almighty Dollar. I can't really explain to them in a way they'd understand why it's so damned important, can't tell them about the law of last best chances, about having to land someone before the bait's all gone. They wouldn't understand it.

Maybe, more to the point, they'd misunderstand it, thinking I was suggesting I had to settle for Michael, and then they'd be forced to spring to my defence, telling me there was no need to settle for anything. Or anyone.

Look, pragmatism may not cancel out faith, but it does make absolutely sure there's not one single thing left to chance. Maybe you don't make luck, but you sure can give it every possible chance to happen. To me, the equation's pretty simple: if I sell this house for enough money, I've got something extra to offer. Sure, it's the only nest egg that I've built up myself, something I should get to depend on, but it can't hurt to have it there in the bank, to even things up if Michael ever starts trying to balance things out—if Michael ever starts doing the math, adding up who brought what to the equation, who made what sacrifice, who paid the most, who brought the most. If he ever does, then with the house money I hope we'll be closer to square. Math happens, and it usually happens when there's already a fight going on, and by then it's always too late to redraw the lines.

Besides, the sale of the house, written on the essential napkin, is my part of the deal. That means it's kind of cast in stone in the alchemy of our relationship. Sometimes you have to keep those things because there's just so little else.

I want to take the girls and shake them until they under-stand—and at the same time, I don't want them to ever have to understand this at all, because I want all of it to pass right over them without ever touching them. They deserve a future that's simple and clean, not this. I want to save them from it completely, so that neither of them ever has to understand the despair that comes with falling down and getting up, only to be knocked back down again by love's bitter backhand. The jarring, despairing clatter of always winding up back at the starting point, hands empty, arms slack at my sides, elbows loose, face bare and looking upwards.

They're on the edge of adulthood, both of them—Eva sixteen and Sarah eighteen—and their heads should be full of summer jobs and university and the inevitable crushing crisis of lost or abandoned boyfriends. Or even girlfriends— I wouldn't mind that either. They shouldn't have to be trying to keep me cemented together and whole and on track, shouldn't be virtual slave labour in their own personal house-flip show. They shouldn't be cleaning and scrubbing and getting ready to start packing again.

But tomorrow we have to paint, regardless. It takes two days for the smell of new paint to fade, even if I've got the dehumidifier going. Real estate agents know all about fresh paint; their noses bring them right to it, like a ferret to a rat, and that always leads to questions.

There are showings scheduled for Thursday, and by then the house has to look like someplace else. It has to be the kind of dream that makes newlyweds grab each other's shoulders and whisper that they have to have this place, even if I know that it's all staged, like a specialized and carefully drawn lie.

Hello fly, my name is spider.

I'm outside having another angry cigarette, and I've got the portable phone out at the very edge of its technically possible universe. Even one foot more and the dial tone will just simply fade, leaving only my own voice ringing back at me through the handset, with a flat echoing sound like talking into a big empty cardboard box. Out here on the back deck, the phone is creating its own nimbus of sound, its own aural aurora borealis. It's full of pops and snaps of static, random fugitive electricity, so it sounds like I'm calling him from Borneo, even though we're only on different sides of St. John's. The serene and temperate continent of Shaw Street is calling the distant island nation of Forest Road. Sometimes you want to be an island, your own whole continent, just so you can keep your coastlines clear, with someone always up high, marking the horizon for the arrival of unexpected strangers.

Listening to the crackling phone, I imagine all the electricity leaking out of the houses around me through cracks and fissures—snatches of fights, recriminations, all of it sinking into me like microwaves; that someone will break in on the phone line at any moment and snarl "Go fuck yourself," and I'll have no idea who it is or whom they're saying it to, but the tone will still make me shiver as if they'd said it directly to me.

Michael's probably downtown, probably on another bitter little kicked-out tear around the downtown bars. He's raw right now. "Sometimes," he said to me, "it just feels like I've pitched forward off a bike onto the pavement and ripped off every square inch of my skin, and now the salt truck's going by."

I know that feeling too. I've had it more than once, recognize parts of it as if it were symptoms of a cold—headache first, then runny nose—but I don't rub Michael's nose in it. I think it's probably better for him to work through it all himself.

I see him every day because we work together, so it's not like I can't keep an eye on him and monitor all the symptoms. "Mary Wells, relationship nurse, understanding is our specialty."

Mary Wells Furneaux for eight years, Stan Pender's "partner" for a few years after that, then Paul Reid's long-time, long-suffering girlfriend—nothing else ever offered or, really, expected. Not from him.

Just Mary Wells now.

I tell myself I can stay on the phone for exactly as long as my cigarette lasts, and then it's back to work.

I know he's on the run now, fugitive and hard to pin down. Intellectually, I know he's got to get through a whole bunch of stuff on his own without me hanging on his shoulder. Problem is, I'm not always intellectual. Sometimes, emotional, human Mary just wants someone's arms wrapped around her.

I phone him again anyway. The machine again. "Leave a message."

I think of all the messages piling up in there like little pink electronic slips in a box, in careful chronological order. Like geological layers smacked down in the silt and then compressed, so some scientist could dispassionately look at them all later and chart the changes in tone, the elevating stress levels in my voice. I picture a graph projected on a screen, and a serious man in a lab coat aiming a pointer at an ever-increasing red line. "At this point, you can see the first signs of the real pathology developing . . ."

"Michael." I say it just like that. Full stop, like I'm a telegraph operator sending out a careful message in an obscure and little-known code. "I hope you're all right. I hope you're having fun. I've got the girls working like dogs in the bathroom, and I need some advice."

Much more formal, staccato this time, the lab coats would note, crabbed handwriting in small field notebooks whose pages take ink even in the pouring rain. Well, fuck all the scientists and their notes and their experiments too.

Stop, inhale, not too hard, breathe out again, smoke up all around my face like my mouth has suddenly turned incandescent and any words that come out of it will scorch.

"I'm thinking I should strip down the border around the living room, put a lighter one up." I don't know why I'm even talking to him about it, because things like this, he doesn't have a clue. Family law he knows—but decorating? I might as well be talking to a post.

Michael's been a lawyer for twenty years or so, a partner now, and I work with him at the firm. "The firm"—that's almost funny. Williams, Carter and Wright, Family Law, three lawyers in a downtown street-front walk-up, two secretaries and one dogsbody—me.

"We've got the basement completely cleaned out now, and the driveway's piled up with stuff. I don't know if the garbage truck's even going to take it all, so I was thinking—"

Click. The machine dismisses me. I've overstayed my electronic welcome again. I could call back to finish the thought, but why bother? I'd just make it abundantly clear that I'm performing the desperation chorus, a song sung in many parts by one voice—and all of them are mine. The thought of it makes my throat clench, and I fumble another cigarette out of the pack, even though I've only just flicked the last butt out into the grass.

I've got to remember that too, before Thursday: rake the yard. A forest of cigarette butts is an easy horror to fix. Not like bathroom taps that were installed badly and don't come off as easily as they're supposed to. That was three hours of work that I didn't even have on my list, and it gave me bleeding knuckles, too.

Later, I can't find the phone. When I do, it's on the railing outside, and it's like a dead thing, completely cold to the touch.

We haven't slept together at his apartment yet. His office, yes, and in the hotel across the street, and even a few times at my house. But his apartment is sacrosanct, like a vestry or something, right now. I even called it that once, "the vestry," just joking, but it went right past him, and he sat there blinking at me as if the words didn't make any sense.

He keeps saying he wants to invite me over there for dinner, but he hasn't yet. I think he's building it in his head into something more momentous than it should be, charging the event up with all kinds of impending expectations that are really only guaranteed to make it fail. It would be simpler if we just fell into his apartment, if we just drove by and he said, "Why don't you come in?" but I think we're past offhand

and into that curious preserve where every single thing is suddenly fraught. He's expecting perfect, trying almost to manufacture it through sheer force of will, and that's exactly where things always start to crash and burn.

The first time we slept together—okay, the first time we had sex—was almost by accident. You have to let things happen—just let them happen. Preparation? Lawyers call it *mens rea*, the guilty mind, the fact that you know something is wrong and make it happen, go ahead with it anyway. But it wasn't something I was planning, even though I knew things between him and Beth were rocky. I really don't think it was something he was expecting either.

As trite as this sounds, we were working late, and in a romance novel it would be "and then we touched," and the fact is that we did, the outside of his left wrist on the inside of my arm as I put a case file in front of him, and that was all it really took. I can forget a lot of things, just let them slide out of my head, but I'll never forget that touch, the way it shot right through me, an unexpected antidote to restraint, and an overdose at that.

It was the kind of explosion where clothes get ripped and the tender, confused part is all in the afterwards—when the drugs wear off and you find that you've actually wound up in a different place. That all the math has changed, and it's almost sad because, when you think about it, you realize that you liked the old math just fine too.

We picked up the files we had knocked off the desk, and then we went at it again on the floor.

There's dignity for you.

Carpet burns, legal files, and hard, fast, intense sex with someone else's husband.

Two in the morning, and the bars aren't even closed, so I shouldn't have to start worrying that he's thrown it all in and gone back to her.

I worry about it anyway. Repeatedly.

What a mess that would be—my house already on the market, my job suddenly in limbo because there's no way she'd have him back with me still hovering around his desk every day, asking him to sign things and ignore the proximity of my breasts. I mean, I'm good at what I do and there's always work for good legal assistants, but this is a small town and the word gets out quick, especially in the legal fraternity. And a fraternity it is, too. A lot of old boys, and they run into each other at court and pass around all the good gossip: which criminal defence lawyer's slipped into a coke addiction, who's on the edge of being caught with their hands in their trust accounts, which member of the esteemed bar has developed a predilection for administering the estates of near-blind old ladies, and charging the old biddies creative fee scales too. And inevitably, who's sleeping with whom.

The day wouldn't be complete without sharing that hot gossip, and I imagine Michael and I are pretty juicy conversation right about now.

The girls have gone to bed, their eyes hollow with a full day of hard work, and I can't imagine it will take them very long to fall asleep. After they're asleep, there's no one left to rein me in, no reason to keep my voice down or anything.

"Leave a message . . ."

I imagine Michael coming home and seeing the red light flashing, a bright little flash for every message, and I imagine him leaping straight through to crisis in his head. With the calls I've made and just hung up, there must be seven or eight flashes on the machine, visual Morse code for "helphelphelphelp." At least, that's the way it would seem to me. Maybe he's already home. Maybe he's picked them all up already. And maybe he's out on his back deck, looking down into the valley over all those roofs and smoking, wondering how to disentangle himself from the arms of a girlfriend who's clearly insane. Maybe he's thinking that a cold, formal marriage is looking a hell of a lot better than someone who's clutching at him all the time, someone who knows better but is doing her damnedest to smother him anyway.

If I was a friend of his, hearing about me, I'd advise him to get away from me as quickly as possible.

The house smells like caulking and I've broken a wineglass, frantically trying to rub shoe scuffs off the bottom of the outside front door. Sometimes the front door sticks at the bottom in the summer. When it's humid, the casing swells, and then we just kick the bottom corner of the door when we turn the knob and push it open.

I've been working out in the cold, the wine next to me, and when I knock the glass, I'm sure it's landed in soft snow, but there it is, all in shards anyway, looking like some kind of special ice. The spilled red wine has left a small stain like piss from a tiny, critically ill dog. A small dog who's lifted his leg in disdain and then disappeared again, too light and fleeting to even leave footprints in the soft, drifted snow. The door's not sticking now, but the little black smears of rubber left by our shoes have defeated every single cleanser until, in frustration, I got out a can of paint thinner from the basement, and that took the marks off—but it took the paint off too, so now I have to repaint. And it's hard to know how well the paint's going to go on in the cold, whether it will even stick, when nothing else in my life ever seems able to. I think my neighbours must be used to seeing me sitting on the front stairs crying by now.

On the phone again. It's after three, and he really should be home. I count each ring with my hopes falling, because it's a small place and he's usually on the phone by the third ring. It gets to four and I'm ready for the machine again when Michael suddenly answers.

He's drunk. Really, really drunk. But that's okay, because it's that nuzzly, needy drunkenness, that warm-blanket, sloppy-kissing, maudlin kind of ardour that topples into snoring before anything really gets going. Luckily, not the screaming "You've destroyed my family, you bitch" kind of drunk, although I'm always waiting, always afraid that might be what I get when he eventually picks up the phone. Put it this way: I hope for "wish you were here" and almost always expect "wish you were gone."

I can hear how drunk he is right away, the way his voice has dropped a full note in the register, the way some of the words have softened at the ends, the consonants losing their shape or just their way. He's got a mild St. John's accent that creeps out when he's had too much to drink. His words are louder too, like the liquor has made him slightly deaf.

"You've had a night, then," he says, the phone held crazily away from his mouth so that he sounds like he's talking on the wall phone in a warehouse.

"So you got all my messages," I say.

"I was going to call, but I was having trouble with my shoes. They seem to have developed a peculiar kind of knots all their own."

And then I hear it. That self-deprecating chuckle that's as much him as his smell is; as much him as where he puts his hands to move me around when we're making love, never speaking, as silent as if it was all as important as ritual.

I don't know why—I want to be angry with him for putting me through the evening, but all at once I feel the frustration vanish, like the dam's burst and it's all just run away right out of me.

"Sounds like you had a night too," I say, suddenly relieved. Everything I needed to talk to him about, well, I don't need to hear about anymore. Security is like an anchor, and I can feel the bow of my ship turning up into the wind, everything safely in place again. "Get some sleep, love, and call me in the morning. When you can."

I know that he's going to be hurting in the morning, that he'll replay all the messages—if he hasn't accidently erased them all—and then will spend the day trying to make amends for my panic. And that will be all right too, because it will be sweet and painful and magical.

Beth's lawyers served him with divorce papers a week after she found out, right after someone called her with one of those helpful anonymous "I just think you should know" calls.

I can't ever let it slip that I know exactly who called her—that it was actually me—and I can't ever let it out, not even when I feel the words trying to bubble urgently up in my throat. Not even when Michael and I are drunk and naked and coiled up together on the bed, post-coital and confessional. I know those words are going to try to escape, no matter how diligently I try to keep them back, because part of me needs him to know how desperately I want him with me. I know that small act is always going to be something that's caught there between us. That's a hard way to start a relationship, with a dirty little secret wrapped up tight and hidden away, when you're supposed to be just getting used to sharing everything. But for me, it's a trade-off. Because I also know about what kind of bad behaviour you can defend and what kind you can't. What you can explain and what you can't. Because everything was down on paper, everything that we were going to do, all on that napkin and agreed to, even if it hadn't been set in motion. I just hadn't expected it to be so hard.

The front door is closed behind me, and I'm leaning my back against the cold metal that I'm absolutely sure will never take paint cleanly again, looking at the pile of garbage on the driveway and thinking about every single thing in there that's made each of the last moves with me.

I hadn't expected that everything would feel like a stone dropped to the bottom of a very deep well.

I'll spend another day painting, and by the time we're done, the girls and I will have the house spotless and as down-right cute as we can, ready to make prospective buyers think about exactly what they can do with every room.

I'll make spice cake on the morning before the open house, and I'll leave it to cool on the counter while we're out.

I hate spice cake.

That's a small—but necessary—secret.

THE GASPER

*D*AVE SIMPSON WAITED. It wouldn't be long, he thought, and he tried to keep his breathing even and slow. That's what they would expect him to do, that's what they would tell him to do. "Just breathe slowly, sir," they'd say, just like that, pumping up the blood pressure cuff and checking his pulse before they even asked his name.

They'd ask his name even if they already knew it. Dave knew the drill—he'd heard it plenty of times before. Different paramedics, but the questions always the same order, the pattern set, Dave was sure, to cut the risk of mistakes. They'd ask a few questions, listen to the answers to try to make sure he was breathing properly, ask him if he was in any pain, where the pain was, and then they'd start the formal workup, one of them putting the details down in their notebook in quick shorthand, the other one with their hands travelling around his body, feeling here, looking there, like they were following a familiar road map.

Dave could feel the rough concrete steps through his pants up against the back of his legs, and against the heels of both of his hands where he'd set his pyramid of body and arms, fixed in place and upright, leaning slightly backwards so that he felt solid. He hadn't fallen. It was important to tell them that he hadn't fallen. They'd ask. Halfway down the hill on Prescott, there were five short steps in the sidewalk because the grade was too steep. He'd just sort of slid down slowly, not letting go of the railing until he was fully settled. He felt like he was some kind of giant advertising balloon, but with a leak, the air running out as he bent and eased down. It was an ordered collapse—no rush, because it was so familiar to him. The air getting short, the edges of everything starting towards dark, and then someone noticing and asking if he needed help. Making the call for him, sending the ambulance on its way from the bay at the Health Sciences Centre.

He had waved her away afterwards, a young woman in a knee-length brown skirt and a square businesslike jacket, her face clearly caught halfway between concern about him and the need to already be somewhere else. She'd half knelt there next to him, one sharp nyloned knee out through the slit in her skirt, a hand on his shoulder briefly as if that short contact was the only first aid she knew how to give, as though mere comfort could be cure. He told her he'd be all right, that he'd be all right to just wait for the ambulance, saying that she could go on, that there "must be other things you've got to be doing." Said it short, in bursts, two or three words at a time, the pauses measured as he tried to catch his breath. People like to help, but they like to be let off the hook too, Dave knew. To know that they've done their duty but can be released from it before anything nasty or messy happens, anything that it might be hard to forget later.

Dave watched the woman walk away, caught her turning once to look at him at the corner of Prescott and Bond, looking back like she was afraid she might see him toppled over on his side. I'd wave if I had enough energy to lift my hand, Dave thought, but he didn't.

He felt the cool air against the damp of his skin. Dave listened to his breath rushing in and out, trying to make each breath come evenly, trying to stay calm, trying to will his throat to open. They'd say that too—"Stay calm, sir, just stay calm"—as if the panic were something you could simply wish away, as if being out of control were as easily dealt with as deciding to be back in control again. But it wasn't that easy.

There was sun in the maples on the other side of the street. Dave squinted over at them and decided he liked the way the light worked through the leaves, the way some were a brighter green—but just for a second—carved up by the light and the shadows of other leaves playing across them, so that the shapes weren't so much maple leaves as they were an assembly of countless and untrackable shards of different leaves, moving across one another in haphazard order. Like there was a message in there, even if the message was that the order everybody is always looking for is just a lie, Dave thought.

He could hear the siren now, distant and a little fractured, like the ambulance was going past occasional square buildings that blocked the rising and falling sound. He tried to imagine the paramedics in the front seats, the way they must

ride along totally used to the sound of the siren, so that it
didn't have any urgency at all, the one in the passenger seat
with a cup of coffee, his body pressed hard up against the
door so that the motion of the ambulance didn't even slop
the coffee over the edges of the cup.

A lot depends on the dispatchers, Dave realized. A lot
depends on how they interpret what they're hearing over the
phone, the sound of his voice on the other end of the line, and
it's not right that their decision should be so subjective—that
they could decide what kind of urgency an ambulance would
have. Dave knew they could make the ambulance just sing—
that they could go on the radio and say a few words and anyone who was riding with a coffee would be rolling down the
window and throwing it outside, coffee and cup and lid and
all, and they'd have their gloves on long before they stopped,
even if the driver had to hold the steering wheel with his
knees while he struggled to push the awkward fingers into
place. And Dave suspected it was better now when he didn't
make the call himself, if someone else took out their cellphone and pressed the three quick buttons, explaining in fast
sentences just what it was they had come across.

He looked around, noticing—as he had before—how
bright the colours were, how every single thing seemed more
distinct and intense. Some part of him checking things off,
sure that this was his last opportunity to gather it all in.
Across the street, there was a cat in a front window, watching
him.

What do cats see through windows? Dave considered it.
Do they think they're looking at a real world, or is it just like

television to them—motion and flat colour and little more? Dave watched the cat stare at him and then look away, uninterested. A man walked by on the sidewalk, fast, talking deliberately on his cellphone, making it clear he had no time to be disturbed. He brushed by where Dave was sitting and didn't look back. Dave was leaning over towards the railing by then, watching the little stars gathering and whirling at the edges of his vision. Little flaring sparkles that you couldn't grasp if you tried to look straight at them. Like a moving frame around his field of vision, and now it was as though he was looking at the street through a long tunnel.

Dave could feel his throat closing over even more; he could feel it as simply as that. He thought this must be like what people feel if they're allergic to bees or peanuts and got that haphazard nut or sting. That clear consciousness, that distinct awareness of your body's betrayal, that few minutes' knowledge that you're the victim of a knee-jerk physical reaction gone all wrong.

Dave watched the ambulance round the corner at the bottom of Prescott Street, and when it did, he felt the weight in his chest lighten a bit, as though his body had realized there wasn't much waiting left, as though it didn't have to steel itself, as if it didn't have to keep rationing air. He watched the staggered flash of the white and red and yellow lights, and he wondered when they'd added the yellow ones; he knew he'd seen them before, he couldn't remember when he'd seen them first. Newer ambulances now, more equip-ment—but you still sometimes got one of the old ones. Dave always looked around the inside of those older ones like he

was recognizing an old friend, full of shiny surfaces and rattling, banging pieces of equipment.

They'd gotten new jackets too, the paramedics, sometime in the past two years. New jackets with a lot more yellow in them, reflective patterns on the back that made the
paramedics stand out garishly like cut-outs of themselves,
especially at night. Dave wondered if they minded being that
obvious, or whether it was like any other uniform—the sort
of thing you didn't mind, because it was a sign of what you
did and where you fit.

Dave could remember when there was a place where he
fit. Not with a single formal uniform as much as with an
understanding of what it was he was supposed to wear. White
or light blue shirts with a collar, a necktie—the more staid, the
better—and pants with a sharp crease. At least, with a sharp
crease first thing in the morning. All of it saying that the
world was under control—in fact, everything was under control, restrained, fastened, buttoned down.

He'd been with the city, in the planning department,
deep into the world of easements and green space. Then
there was a new mayor with a background in business and
a public mantra that the only thing you could really control
was the size of your expenses. Then, everyone was talking
about "the economy contracting," and there began to be
empty desks, although at first it was just the part-timers and
the co-op students.

Dave thought it felt exactly like a contraction: a sharp
muscular squeeze, impossible to resist. Like the world suddenly bore down, pushed, and popped him right straight out

into another, very different place with a week's pay for every year on the job. He remembered how, in the good moments, he'd been sure there would be another job long before the severance ran out.

The moment they'd told him, they were already looking over him, past him and on to the next thing. Dave remembered what it had been like with other layoffs, knew the way everyone else in the room didn't even have time to think about how unfair it was because they were so keenly aware about how glad they were it wasn't happening to them.

Linda hung on for a while. Dave knew she might have stayed in the marriage longer if he'd managed to cut back on their expenses quicker, if he'd looked ahead and asked, "What if something doesn't come along?" But Dave hadn't wanted to do that. It struck him all at once when the severance was almost gone, unemployment insurance looming, and he'd found himself at the checkout in the liquor store, buying exactly the same single malt Scotch he always had. "One small luxury," he had told Linda when he started buying it years earlier, when there was enough of a cushion for tolerance. "That's all I need."

Every evening, he'd have one small glass of the peaty brown Scotch—nothing special about the glass, either, just a juice glass with a single ice cube in it—and thinking back, Dave wondered what was important about it, whether it was the Scotch itself or the idea of it. The idea of going into the living room with the glass, sitting in his chair with the newspaper while the ice cube melted slowly, the ice occasionally splitting with an audible crack, the order of the world set as carefully as if it had been framed up and poured with concrete.

Dave wondered where that chair was now, and he wondered where Linda was too. Neither of them were in the rooming house he shared with six other people, two of them recently released from the mental hospital. Social Services paid Dave's rent but little more, and he found it was easier to be outside walking than to stay in the whirlwind of the house, a place where everything seemed completely beyond his control. If he wanted to read a book, there was no guarantee there wouldn't be someone screaming insults in their room, or knocking on his door to see if he could help with a problem one of the other residents was having with welfare or the landlord. "You know numbers, Dave," would be the half-apologetiç explanation for involving him in something that could take the rest of the day. It was easier to be away from the building, easier to keep his thoughts in their own order.

Dave looked down at his knees, at the grey of his trousers and the grey of the concrete step set into the sidewalk. Any trace of a pleat was gone from the fabric; even something as simple as that was beyond him now. His breathing sharp and short, so that his throat was suddenly dry and sore.

The ambulance was up by the curb, and the two paramedics came out through the doors, and when they saw him, when they recognized him, it was like they lost a half step of urgency. It was a man and a woman, and the man said, "Hi, Dave," as he set the bright orange trauma kit down on the steps. "Same thing, Dave?"

"Hi Tony," Dave said, his breath rasping. "Same thing."

"Didn't know it was going to be you again," the female paramedic said. Her name patch said Patricia, but everyone called her Patty. "We must have brought you in ten times by now."

"Thanks," was all Dave could manage. Then Patty was bringing the gurney from the back of the ambulance, and as they wheeled him to the doors, the clear plastic oxygen mask over his mouth and nose, Dave was surprised at how bright the sky was.

Tony was driving, and Dave heard him jog the radio microphone off its rest into his right hand and call the hospital. "Male, fiftyish, vitals good. Trouble breathing." Then there was a short break, as if Tony was trying to make up his mind about what to say. Looking up from where he was lying on his back, Dave could just make out the shape of the driver against the bright windshield.

"We've got the Gasper, folks," Tony said. "No lights, no siren."

And Dave was sure he heard the resignation in Tony's voice when he said it.

The back of the ambulance was full of the grumble of the big diesel engine and the hiss of the oxygen through the mask. The ceiling light was on, and Dave could see the ambulance rocking left and right as it made its way around corners. He watched Patty's body lean back and forth involuntarily with each turn, watched her muscles brace and relax. She didn't look at him, didn't look at the monitors they had him connected to. Once or twice she looked down at her hands in the blue vinyl gloves, her mouth pursed small, but she didn't say anything.

In ten minutes, they were at the hospital, and the two attendants pulled the gurney out and let the wheels beneath it drop hard into place and lock. Dave watched the roof of the ambulance bay and then the ceiling of the hospital rolling by as he was wheeled into the emergency room. And Tony was talking to the triage nurse, giving her the quick rundown on Dave's symptoms and vital signs. Dave knew enough to know they were treating him differently than they would other patients—no notes, no careful handover with plenty of explanation—and in a way it made him feel smaller.

"We'll take you down to a room until a doctor can see you," the nurse said. "You breathing all right with the oxygen?"

Dave could only nod, not enough air left to even speak, but the intensity was sliding away, as if his bronchial tubes were fingers that he could feel flexing and easing. Now that it was softening, he knew he'd soon be past it.

The doctor was brief—drive-by medicine with other patients to see. "Are you taking your prescription, Mr. Simpson? Because it's pretty clear you're having a panic attack again. You've got to get this under control—you've been here half a dozen times already this month."

Dave didn't tell the doctor that there weren't enough dollars left at the end of the month to keep him in pills, or that he was suddenly entranced by the simple feel of the cool, smooth, clean sheets under the side of his face.

There must have been something about the look on his face then, because the doctor looked up from the chart and stared at him for a moment or two, his face inscrutable. "We're not that busy here today, Mr. Simpson," the doctor said, finishing the chart and hanging it back on the end of the bed, pen quickly back into the pocket on his jacket. "Stay here on the oxygen for a while until you feel up to it. I'll get you discharged after that."

Dave stayed on his side, studying the weave of the sheet, the lines where the threads came together and the tiny holes between. He put his hand out to feel the rough-washed scrape of the fabric and, deciding his fingers wouldn't be able to feel it well enough, turned his hand over and dragged the back of it across the small hills and valleys, caught up in that one action.

Over the gentle hiss of air from his mask, Dave could hear scattered noises from other parts of the emergency room: the clicking of a piece of nearby equipment, a regular beeping sound and, from across the hall, the sound of someone crying. The other hospital is older, Dave thought, but it's quieter. Like the walls are thicker or something—like different things used to be important. St. Clare's was a little more careworn, chipped paint and older beds. It's funny, he thought, to actually be thinking about which hospital you like better.

Half an hour later, one of the nurses brought a small box of apple juice, the L-shaped straw sticking out of the top. "Just check in with us when you're ready to go," she said.

Half an hour after that, the drinking box empty, Dave pulled the oxygen mask off his face and swung his legs down over the side of the bed. When he was outside, he saw three ambulances by the bay, and Tony and Patty had the doors open on theirs, sliding the gurney into the back. He watched for a moment, wavering slightly, and then they saw him. The sun had passed through noon, and Dave squinted to look out across the plain of the parking lot. It was like the sun had gotten whiter while he was in the hospital, the colours of the cars and the trees all flatter than they had been. At least it wasn't raining.

"Cry wolf enough, Dave, and we might not be there when you really need us," Tony said.

Patty spoke up from the other end of the gurney. "The dispatchers all know your voice by now," she said.

"I wouldn't call," Dave said. "I wouldn't call if I didn't have to. But thanks."

He braced himself to start across the parking lot. It would be a long walk, he thought. It always was.

Dave saw a quick look pass between the two, but it was Tony who spoke. "Want a run back downtown, Dave? We're heading to St. Clare's for a patient transfer anyway."

Five days later, he was on Water Street, nursing a large coffee, sitting on a stool in a street-front coffee shop. It was raining, large flat drops blowing in against the glass and sliding down in long streaks.

Dave's eyes focused on the running drops, then on the people passing by, his eyes flicking back and forth as they locked onto the changing images, his attention caught by each individual motion. With every passing pedestrian, he

thought there was a little bit of each face that seemed familiar—not like he knew them in particular, but as if there was
some reason why he thought he should know them. They
passed like water in a river, he thought, heading in their own
directions, each one with their own piece of the world safe
and sound and trusted. He envied them that, whether it was
blind faith or foolish confidence or just plain ignorance.

There's so much you can't control, Dave thought, the
coffee cup warm in his hands, no matter what you think, no
matter how fast you make your way down the street.

Then he felt the sharp shear, the familiar tightening in
his chest.

"Excuse me," he said, smiling up at the waitress. "I'm . . .
I'm not feeling well. Can you call an ambulance?"

I LIKE

*T*HERE IS SO LITTLE left to be dancing for, Keith thought—and when there was dancing, it was him doing soft-shoe in the kitchen, alone, from stove to fridge and back again, getting out an onion, a carrot, the lemons.

Somewhere in the wall, the water was running, a hissing rush he knew better than most other sounds in the house. Was it the pipes that made the sound, he wondered, or the choke point of the tap, toning the pressure down? When it was flowing, the sound of the water radiated from the pipes to wherever he was in the house, so that anything from the dishwasher to the shower could make its own throat clearing and steady comment.

Funny, he thought, how sounds can actually seem accusing.

It was Anna in the shower, washing the angry right down into her skin. The water so hot that she'd come out branded in red blotches across her back, marked with flags combining her penitent frustration with slowly developing fury.

Once, he would have listened for that shower, for those
sentinel calling pipes, like a bloodhound scenting lost children, his face high towards the ceiling, his head turning back
and forth to triangulate the sound, just so he could rush up
the stairs to join her, pulling his sweatshirt over his head as
he took the stairs two at a time. Opening the bathroom door
because knocking was unnecessary, just like invitations were.
She would be expecting him anyway, obeying a kind of naked
hunger that neither of them was remotely embarrassed
about. Dancing together through the curtain of drops. Wet
rhythm, tango, rumba. Tile-rattling, grout-gripping pas de
deux.

Anna was always eager in a way that pulled him right out
of himself. With Anna, he thought, you might start out self-
conscious and self-aware, but the concept of being separate
and self-contained melted away quickly.

They'd met in university and had somehow managed to
hang on through that curious gap when graduates suddenly
change from moving in one similar direction to casting out
along their own individual routes. Keith couldn't help but
think that staying together was mostly her doing, that she
had managed against serious odds to drag him through with
her, an alchemy made easy by the lure of all that raw desire.

Anna, with her intense face caught in a tight frame of short
blond hair. A woman who'd always had a penchant for hiding herself inside clothes large enough to be someone else's,
a woman you found like a small and important discovery.

She had planned on postgraduate work in English, but
when the fellowship didn't come through, she'd wound up

as a newspaper reporter, doomed to the entertainment beat and the crushing duty of interviewing up-and-comers who were always on their way to somewhere else while Anna stayed solidly, pointedly, in the same place.

Keith, at one time, carried a brief fantasy of heading somewhere, almost anywhere, else. He'd toyed with the idea of the police or the military, and ended up turning sideways into a surprisingly simple job inspecting elevators and pressurized tanks for the provincial government. The inspections were so routine he couldn't remember the last time one of the pieces of equipment had actually failed: a page or two of copied visual inspection reports, with boxes to check off and the occasional single line for a written comment. There was the all-important space at the bottom to mark and initial, but only after the fee was paid.

Keith could work all day and then be completely unable to remember the location of the last building he'd been in, the work stretching out behind him in a seemingly endless collection of cables, grease, pulleys and confined spaces. When someone lost something down the crack between the elevator car and the shaft, they never, ever went looking for it. It was like people were expecting something unknown in the dark—monsters under the bed. So Keith found change and keys and sometimes toys at the bottom of any number of elevator shafts, abandoned because asking for help was too much trouble.

For a while, Keith's and Anna's jobs—because they *were* jobs, not anything like careers—were enough, as long as there was also home and the sheer probability of each other's arms. When he thought about it, Keith guessed that Anna was probably less comfortable with what they had settled for than he was, less satisfied with the way things had worked out, and it reared its head in strange ways. Every month, new solutions had to be found for the problems that cropped up between them, problems that he wasn't even aware existed until she mentioned them.

Problems with work he could handle. Hers were editors who were bastards or who demanded more work than they were willing to pay for, days that were so long she ended up bringing home one of the portable computers from the office so they could at least be in the same house while she pounded out the last few details of a story before she could file it to the news desk. Harder for Keith to comprehend were the problems between them. It was always a revelation to him when it turned out they had issues that he hadn't even started to consider, that he hadn't even known were there. He knew it was probably a weakness of his—knew it because she told him it was—and thought he must be skating without ever thinking about testing or measuring the emotional ice beneath them, that he didn't spend enough time considering where they were going. Anna saw much better where the rough edges came together, he thought.

When they had time, they'd talk about it, and Anna would outline the problems and detail the possible solutions, and he'd agree desperately every time, worried that the best of his intentions did nothing but set them both up for more crushing falls.

"You just don't get it, do you?" she'd say, exasperated, words like hands thrown up in the air. She'd explain and he'd listen, but the sentences seemed to come out in a foreign language he didn't understand.

Afterwards, both of them would tread carefully, circling each other, moving slowly like they were driving on an unfamiliar road at night and trying not to pile into the unanticipated, last-moment potholes.

But they had muddled along until they married, anyway. Then they bought a house that backed onto a uniform hill capped with a line of Gower Street rowhouses, all the houses the same height, all knit together at their tops, a unison of roofs. Keith supposed that any anchor could be a good mooring. Then again, he didn't really know much about boats.

The kitchen was at the back of the house, and while washing dishes, Keith would watch the sky darken over the row of homes opposite, knowing even when there was nothing left except the glow of their windows that, barring complete catastrophe, they would always be there. The rooflines weren't straight, but they sagged in the same places every single morning and evening, and he found a particular comfort in that.

Once, they argued about paint colours for the front hall and the living room, Anna definite and Keith confused, because he thought he hadn't said anything. In an argument-that-wasn't-really-an-argument (because, he thought, neither of them was disagreeing, really) he found himself reaching out to touch the existing paint, as if trying to feel with his fingertips just why it was that the existing colour couldn't suit, as if there were some mystery wrapped up in there that physical contact would surely let him discover. Anna shouted that if it was the painting he was so damned worried about, she'd do it all.

As weeks went by, and then months, he found himself more and more alone in the kitchen at the back of the house and not really minding, and he tried to tell himself that Anna's work was getting harder, more time-consuming, and that she really didn't like cooking anyway. He did like cooking, more and more, testing and trying, smelling and tasting.

While he worked over the stove, he tried to rationalize that it really was all right if they each moved around in their different spheres, barely touching, keeping different hours so that their clocks only overlapped for a rushed hour or two in the evenings. He told himself it was all right even if, when he ran upstairs to the shower, he somehow didn't feel as welcome with her, or sometimes didn't welcome the opportunity. Keith forced himself not to think about that even on those days when the shower ran especially long, when he knew it was her way of beckoning, carefully unspoken and noncommittal, so that no one would have to lose face. So that no one would have to acknowledge needs unmet or unrecognized, unintentionally edged with a smudge of shame.

He was aware of it anyway from the delicate moue of disappointment she'd have in one corner of her mouth when she came downstairs. It was an expression she would not really know she was making and one he would flatly refuse to recognize. He'd know at the same time that he could gleefully and maliciously play dumb, and that she'd feel wounded without being able to clearly find anyone to blame for the hurt.

Alone, before she came downstairs, he would find a small and visceral release in cutting through the thin tubes of green onions, the sharp tang of their smell rising around his carefully busy hands like mist from damp, bare soil. He didn't know whether it was the onions or the knife or the distance in his expression that kept her away when she finally came downstairs, arms still ruddy from the hot water, turning her face away and searching the fridge for the white wine before heading back up the stairs. But something clearly did keep her away, and he didn't even really notice for long, especially when there were several things cooking at once, the burners lit up glowing red and the steam rising.

He had taught himself to cook out of a mixture of curiosity and necessity—a cup of each, he thought, then stir gently with the whites of two eggs. Necessity, because they had to eat, and it had become clear that no one else was really interested in cooking. Curiosity, because cooking seemed both earthy and magical; something would develop that was so clearly not a product of mere ingredients and temperature and careful attention to the military order of recipes. Later, there would be the addition of a touch of frustrated sensuality, hinted at in fractional scents and flavours, added in infinitesimal amounts like saffron or some other impossibly expensive spice.

Keith started with the simple recipes he remembered from growing up: onion-rich tomato sauces, heavy with garlic and flaked oregano, then thick lasagna and a rich beef stew simmered in brown gravy all day long, heavy chunks of potato and hints of red wine and flat, strong bay leaves. The kinds of things he could remember his mother making without ever looking at a cookbook, as if recipes were written under her skin like a web of small, broken, insistent capillaries.

Then he moved on to longer, more complicated experiments. Soon he had a small block of slab bacon, double smoked, well travelled and wrapped tight in several layers of plastic, buried in the freezer so that he could shave off just a few thin slices to hide in the very beginning of sauces. Mushrooms: white button first, then porcini, then the complication of oyster mushrooms, balancing both taste and texture.

Different specialty vinegars, lined up in the back of the cupboard like a spectrum of similar but slightly distinguishable moods. He moved dinner back a half-hour or so to have more time to prepare, but Anna didn't seem to mind. She simply swallowed the whole half-hour up with work, and never reached a point where she couldn't stand the hunger.

In the process of cooking, he found that even the simple things became more complicated, more layered, more involved. He loved the way the onions changed, the heat under the pan working on sugars you couldn't even taste in the raw, sharp bulbs, a caramelized brown that appeared only over heat. First it was all the onion cousins: yellow, Spanish, vidalia, pearl. Stuck-up shallots. Then it was the close-knit and exotic rice family: arborio, jasmine, basmati.

It was like meeting the relatives one at a time over days, each one slightly more peculiar than the one you'd met just before: one minute, meeting a long-grained mother-in-law with perfectly placed hair and a rigid, accepting smile; the next moment, being introduced to a wizened, blossoming uncle who had no children but who collected model trains, and who ran those trains regularly and hard and alone on their steel rails all night until their small working engines made the air smell like steel wool pressed tight up under your nose.

Keith even liked to roll the different food names around in his mouth, as if the words themselves were flavours or curious, half-recognized scents, five-spice and fennel and licorice, oily anise. He introduced himself to the curious cult and range and temper of the hot peppers. Anna didn't really seem to care; he could chatter away about the different ways he'd looked at a cooking problem and she took it in as if he were talking about different weights of elevator cable.

At parties, though, he found he could talk about food with anyone, and people would either understand or just bask in the idea of it. By then Keith had a row of expensive knives, raw steel blades with their own patina, carefully oiled, always washed by hand because the dishwasher would make them sprout rust on the very first trip; sharp knives that could leave a cut on your finger as fine as a thread, a cut the knives seemed to relish making, a cut that only slowly learned to ooze blood.

Then the night came when he was making a wine sauce with black peppercorns, watching the wine darkening and purpling in the silver of the pan, and wondering if buying a gas range would be a ridiculous suggestion to make with money still so tight. The peppercorns looked invincible and still dry in their black and wrinkled armour, woody and impervious, as if they were intent on giving up nothing about themselves despite the torture; and the alcohol from the wine boiled off into the air in a wave that made Keith shiver when it caught in his nose and stopped his breath.

Anna was leaning in the doorway with her wineglass again, rejoining the campaign, looking at him. And Keith wondered if she had realized, at that very moment, how formal they had become with each other, the way they had learned to keep artificial spaces around themselves, moving to the sides of the hall when they passed each other, as if they were almost strangers. He'd been noticing it for weeks, like a hint of varnish in the air, even though nothing had been painted.

Being the first to notice it felt somehow wrong, because it occurred to Keith all at once that it should have been her recognizing the circles they'd built around each other. It had always been her job to see the shadows long before he did; it was as if she had fallen down on the job. Keith couldn't decide if he'd fallen in the shower and struck his head or if she'd fallen from the watchtower where she was supposed to be safely overlooking their lives.

As he watched, Anna drank, the glass nearly empty now, her eyes measuring as she looked back at him.

The wine sauce was boiling unheeded, spattering over the edge of the pot, tiny droplets landing on the hot white enamel and annealing themselves into flat black specks instantaneously, their presence not even visible in the air until they were fixed in place on the stove, the circular pattern forming around the pot becoming more complete with each passing moment.

On the back burner, a big iron pot was heating languidly, a pool of olive oil splitting apart into droplets on top of the water and then rejoining in a green and round-edged blob. Whenever he picked up the lid of the pot, he could smell the feral rich breath of trees in the oil. Next to that pot there was broccoli, still green and cold in the steamer, slivered almonds to go over the top like unexpected snow.

She reached her hand out towards him then, her palm down and fingers spread, the rest of her arm so straight it looked as if her elbow were on the verge of bending backwards too. All in one—invitation, supplication, desperation.

Keith realized he was holding a wooden spoon out in front of him like a short sword, a pot lid in his other hand like a shield, and all he really needed was a colander for a helmet and he'd be back in grade four, calling fellow soldiers to suit up from the armoury in the drawer under the stove. He realized that he felt exactly like a nine-year-old, felt as if he should have his lower lip stuck firmly out.

"So, maybe I've been working too hard," Anna said as Keith put the spoon and lid down, and she set her wineglass on the kitchen table. "Smells good."

It came out short, like an admission, as if prised out against her will, like ground given. Or deliberately surrendered. Then she pulled his hand up to her lips, kissed it, and smiled.

"Onions," she said.

"Poached with mushrooms in balsamic vinegar," he started. "They're in the fridge for a salad . . ."

She reached a finger across, put it on his lips. "Okay," she said, her voice dropping two quick notes at the end of the word, final and full stop.

He smelled soap on her hand and something else, something high and sharp, like new leather or the bright salt of beach rocks, but a smell he remembered immediately and jarringly as distinctively hers. It had been a long time since he had smelled it. Smelled it and known it.

Anna had the fingers of her left hand woven through his, familiar and cool and smooth and right, the feel of them running through him like a signal coursing through wires.

The windows were all dark by then, and the blue had bled right out of the sky so that the houses opposite, even the last matte black edge of their roofs, had finally vanished. The whole row dark, like every eye was resolutely and deliberately closed, carefully paying no attention at all. Keith knew the houses were all still out there, was absolutely certain of it, each one of them holding its simple truth, out of sight and waiting. And that every one would be there the next morning, surfacing with the rising sun. That there was trust in some anchors, set careful, deep and solid.

He turned off each of the burners and followed her, counted every step of the stairs. As they passed through each doorway, he thought of tumblers falling into place in combination locks—and of walking along the top of a fence, one foot in front of the other, and the tremulous, careful way you have to watch a roux to be sure the butter won't suddenly and angrily brown then burn.

Later, there was the soft feel of cotton against his skin, and the quickening of breath, and Keith felt himself coming all apart into shards of images, sound and smell and sentences that flashed through his mind like scraps cut out at random and glued down on construction paper.

Onions, garlic, limes, smooth skin, urgent hip, the swell of lower lip.

Sugar hunkering down over low heat, crystals slowly softening and surrendering their shape—butter melting, shifting silent from waxy solid to easy slip.

Wait, wait, be patient—wait until the water reaches the necessary, and rolling, boil.

Apples, sharp vinegar, crushed basil, sea salt and iodine.

Salt, like sweat. Like tears.

ACKNOWLEDGEMENTS

I write in a combination of doubt, wonder, fear and occasional confidence, and would not be able to write at all without the help of those who believe in and support my work and also who help tamp down the occasional darkness.

Leslie Vryenhoek edited all these stories and knows them inside out; Pam Frampton, as always, was a crucial first reader.

At Thomas Allen Publishing, Senior Editor Janice Zawerbny and Publisher Patrick Crean continue their constant support. My agent, Shaun Bradley at Transatlantic Literary Agency, fought me out of many corners.

My boys, Peter and Philip Wangersky, and Raquel Bracken once again tolerated the peaks and valleys of having not one but two writers in the house.

Thanks as well to the Newfoundland and Labrador Arts Council and the Canada Council for the Arts, both of which have helped support my work financially.